The Painting 2

By Kathleen J. Shields

Kathleen J. Shields

ISBN-13: 978-1-941345-32-0 Paperback

ISBN-E: 9780463161098 Smashwords

Canyon Lake, TX
www.ErinGoBraghPublishing.com

Foreword

Time changes all things...

There was a fun game that children used to play a long time ago... before technology changed the rules. It was called "Telephone."

The rules were simple. Gather a group of friends into a line. The first person in the line whispers something into the second person's ear. That person has to listen carefully because there are no repeats. They then have to turn to the third person in line and repeat what they heard.

As the story is whispered down the row, it changes. In a couple minutes time, depending on the difficulty of the first phrase, the subject, description or even the entirety of the sentence may change completely. It was quite funny to hear how something can morph and change in a few moments time.

Imagine what that story would turn into over the course of many, many generations. This is what happened in the Painting.

Gerald's story is quite unique though.

What he created defied nature and reality. It shouldn't have worked. He pulled and used a power from the depths of his soul that was not at all possible. Creating a real-live world from paint is something most people couldn't even begin to wrap their heads around. So Gerald's 'telephone' story changed and morphed to fit their beliefs and highly active imaginations.

Over time, over the years, through each generation, a story was told. The painter became the creator. His canvas became his world. The bucket of water that doused the fire became the great flood and his initials: G.O.D. that no one could find any longer, became the spoken name; Geody.

What follows is Gerald's 'telephone' story and how his son, Benjamin, visits the painting in hopes of correcting some of the misconstrued details of his father's greatest masterpiece.

Chapter 1

True Love is a feeling of complete peace.
It happens when you open yourself up to the possibility.
It is a complete acceptance, an understanding.
It is pure. It comes from the heart.
It is enchanting.

- *K*

Gerald wasn't alone any longer. He had found friendship. He was part of someone else's life. He had created his own world--a beautiful, enchanting world that was so magnificent and perfect, it needed to be protected. So he put everything he had left into the creation of a universe in which to protect his painting.

His hopes and dreams still flowed from him into the Painting and the emotions still flowed from it into him. He could hear and feel the people within. He could feel their happiness, joys and pleasure, but he could also feel their hurts, sorrows and sadness.

He wanted nothing more than for them to be happy and enjoy this world; find the peace within its perfection. But as *their* years passed by, things began to change.

Time worked very differently in the Painting. One day outside in Gerald's world was a year within the Painting. Every four minutes Gerald watched a day and a night go by. Every minute, more and more people were born into his world. Every few hours a generation expired. Every single day the story of what he created changed.

By the time Gerald had become an adult, married and had a child of his own, the Painting's population had multiplied a thousand times.

Two people became four. Four people became eight. Eight became sixteen, then thirty-two, sixty-four, and over one hundred. A hundred became a thousand, and a thousand soon turned into a million and the story of where 'we' came from? Well that seemed to be one of the first philosophical questions a curious child would ask as they gazed up into the night sky and tried to count the stars.

The twinkling of those tiny white dots that speckled the darkness of space enthralled the curious nature of a child whose favorite questions happened to begin with 'why?'

Why is the sky blue? Why's the grass green? Why do the birds sing? What else is out there?

The answers, while ever changing with intelligence, always tended to have a similar theme.

"The sky is the blue that *he* painted. That shade of green is what *he* wanted. The birds sing because *he* thought it would be beautiful. The creator is out there. He watches over us through those twinkling stars. He smiles at us the way I smile at you," a parent would say as their child glanced up to see the twinkle in their eyes.

It was a beautiful life, a wonderful time to be alive - but there were some who didn't believe.

Chapter 2

"That's ridiculous!"

"But it's the truth."

"Says' who?"

"My grandfather told me. He told my mom who also told me. So it has to be true."

"Who told your grandfather?"

"His parents did. It's been a story that's been passed down over generations."

"That's the point," The person countering would grin, "it's a story. It's make-believe."

"That's not what I meant."

"It's a fairytale your family told you so you would go to sleep at night."

"That's not true!" Jeffrey felt the burning tears welling up in his eyes.

"It is. You are just too gullible." Franklin's lips spread into a cruel smile.

"I am not. My parents wouldn't lie to me. He IS the creator. He made everything and we should thank him for it."

"Well, until I meet him, I'm not going to believe it." Franklin turned and walked away with his head held a tad bit higher after winning this debate.

"One day you'll see." Jeffrey's voice cracked as a single tear slid down his cheek. He wiped it away with the back of his hand and turned to walk home. He believed so strongly and yet couldn't change one person's mind. As he walked, he wondered, is my acceptance of the Painter's creation strong enough?

He was deep in thought when a rustling in the trees to his left caught his attention. At first, he was startled. He thought to run home, but the trees rustled again and this time, his eyes focused on what was causing it.

"Hello big guy." Jeffrey spoke calmly as he slowly walked towards the deer. The large buck had gotten his antlers tangled in the branches of a downed tree. He pulled and yanked trying to free himself but was only getting himself more tangled and bringing attention to his plight.

Jeffrey lifted his hands and cooed a calm "Shhhh..." as he whispered in a low voice, "it'll be okay. Let me help you." He stepped closer, so very slowly, until he was right by the deer.

He could see the buck was terrified. Large animals could be very dangerous when they are scared, he knew this, but he also knew this guy needed his help. He slowly laid a hand on the deer's head. The frightened buck yanked back as hard as he could but the branches snagged his antlers and yanked him back in place.

Jeffery backed away just a step to give the buck a chance to catch his breath. His eyes were wide open; his breathing was heavy and staggered. Jeffrey could sense the deer's heart was racing.

He grabbed a tree branch near the buck's head and broke it. The loud snap startled the deer but again he couldn't escape. Jeffrey snapped another branch. After the third branch, broken and tossed to the side, the deer began to realize what was happening, he was getting helped by this young little boy.

He watched Jeffrey diligently as he worked. Some of the branches were too big to break. Some of them were too fresh to snap. Jeffrey worked hard to lift them and untangle them and move them to the side.

He had his hands on the buck's antlers. They were almost under him as he began maneuvering the sharp horns out of the tangled mess - this he knew was incredibly dangerous. If the buck gets free and lifts those pointy antlers quickly and forcefully, they could impale Jeffrey. He could be stabbed and left for dead!

Now, even Jeffrey's heart was racing. He pressed the antlers down and the branches up. The deer could sense the boy was helping him but his head and neck hurt. His antlers were heavy and they were being pushed and yanked on. He was tired and yet the adrenaline was keeping him energized.

Finally, Jeffrey got some air between the last antler and the brush. The buck yanked backwards and tumbled out of the trees. Jeffrey lost his footing and fell onto the pile. Quickly though, he turned to the buck who soon realized he was free.

The buck steadied his legs; he lifted his head up high. His antlers were much larger than they seemed when they were tangled in the brush. He looked at Jeffrey lying on the pile, then winked and walked away.

He walked away slowly and Jeffrey couldn't help but marvel at the beauty of this majestic beast. As the buck neared the edge of the grove of trees, he looked back at Jeffrey and just stared at him for a moment. Their eyes met and held for a long moment, a moment that filled Jeffrey with great satisfaction. Then the buck leapt out into the sunlight and galloped across the field.

Jeffrey felt like a hero. Jeffrey felt like a hero. A pride filled within him as he had never saved a life before. He had heard stories of how the Painter wanted the people to tend to the animals, to take care of his creations. A smile spread across his face as he began to maneuver himself off of the pile of tree branches. Tumbling to the ground, he laughed.

A clumsy hero, but a hero nonetheless.

Chapter 3

Gerald Oliver Delaney truly enjoyed staring at the universe painting that hung on the wall in his den. It used to hang on his bedroom wall but he had grown up. It had been a long time since he moved out of his parents' home. He now had a home of his own. He married his best friend, Tiffany, and they even had a son.

Gerald's life had turned out much different than what he expected. Of course, he hadn't expected much at all growing up. He had always been so lonely, but now, he was happy.

As he leaned back in his recliner and watched the planets of his universe spiral around the sun, he let his memories take him back to the Painting, the original creation of his world. He'd get lost in his memories.

He could feel the sun warming his face, the cool breeze blowing against his cheeks. He could smell the flowers and salty sea air. He could hear the birds singing, the chipmunks chattering and the wolves howling.

He remembered how peaceful and beautiful it was, and how comforted and welcome he felt there. He fondly recalled the soft white paw of the bunny that had been so curious about him. How the bunny's nose twitched as it sniffed Gerald's face and how its whiskers tickled his nose.

He thought about the people he painted into his world, his likenesses. He thought about how small they were, how curious and brave.

They trusted him with everything. They knew he would take care of them. They knew he would always watch over them.

Gerald heard them talking. He heard them as they lived their lives, as they became friends, as they fell in love, and as they had children.

He felt their joy as their first child was born, then their second. He rejoiced with them for every birthday and anniversary. He was with them as they worked the land, tended to the animals and built their lives.

He was a part of them as their children grew up, and their children had children. He witnessed the world evolve and change. He was a happy spectator beholding the growth of his magnificent world.

The population grew quickly. Towns were created. People spread out, built their homes outside of town. Some went so far away they started their own towns. More people ventured out that way. Those towns grew, so some went even further out.

Before long the entire planet had been occupied. Gerald found it amazing to observe the evolution of his world.

Some people lived up north where it snowed. They created warmer clothes, thicker walls to their homes and very creative ways to travel with the help of the animals that inhabited the land. Their skin was pale and very white because the cold temperatures tended to keep them inside and out of the sun. They almost blended in to their environment. They fished and shipped foods in from other places of the world.

Some people lived around the center of the planet where the sun shined longer and brighter. They were hot most of the time and wore much thinner clothes. Their skin tanned a golden brown, and their hair darkened. Their homes were made of thin thatched plants and they ate the fruit that grew plentifully on the trees surrounding them.

Some people lived much further south where the sun beat down upon the land. There was a lot of sand and very little trees. The animals of the land were larger and ferocious. They evolved to find ways to store water, to survive. The humans were much darker here. They were stronger and valiant. They hunted and herded the animals.

Each area of the planet created new and varied kinds of people. Each group lived differently and each group told their own individual stories of the creator.

Gerald giggled as he listened to the varying stories. He couldn't help but smile as the details changed. Each culture and civilization added their own unique flair to the story; some called him a painter, others a creator. Some described him as the grand designer, the architect of the universe, the author and even the inventor.

His painting, or his world, was formed of clay, constructed of love or established as the symbol of perfection. Each generation added their own style to the story, embellishing upon the legend until Gerald was a mysterious being whose enchantment held the glory of the moon and the stars.

Then there was the universe. The expansion of space and stars and planets, was almost more than most of the world could comprehend. To most, the story of him placing the Painting within the universe didn't make sense.

How could one person do this? A person can no less pick up a tree with his bare hands and move it. So how can an entire world be repositioned inside of a universe that one can't even touch?

Gerald's love was unexplainable, enchanting, and thrilling. Some found it inspiring while others found it terrifying. An omnificent being so powerful he could control the vastness of space? That fear, was what started the chaos.

As the people shared the story, their fears were added to it. "Geody could squash you like a bug if he so desired."

"Fear him, for it was his wrath that flooded the world."

These stories saddened Gerald. He wished he could go back and explain that it was an accident, a mistake. He was just trying to put out the fire, to help and protect the people. But he couldn't go back into the Painting, it was impossible, *now*.

However, he could will the people to listen to his heart. He could give them the desire to correct the story, or to instill a feeling of togetherness - that he did this for the good of everyone. But he couldn't force them to listen to him or believe it.

The arguments began.

The people would disagree with each other. It would cause separation between townsfolk and families. It was horrible.

Chapter 4

"What's wrong daddy?" Little Benjamin would ask his father, Gerald, as tenderly as only a four- year old could do.

"They don't understand, but you do, don't you son?" Gerald patted his lap, encouraging his son Benjamin to come sit with him.

Benjamin smiled at his father. He couldn't wait to come listen to another great story about his father's magnificent world.

"The canvas needed color and the color needed depth and the world needed life and the life needed love. This was how it began and that was how I painted it."

Benjamin curled into a small ball on his father's lap and listened with intent curious wonder. He loved hearing the stories. He heard them every day. Of a father's love, of a creator's will, of a painter's promise.

"Today a young boy saved a deer." Gerald smiled looking deep into his son's adoring eyes. "He risked his own safety to save the life of one of my animals. I felt the fear within him building. He was afraid he was going to get hurt but he knew he had to do this. He knew in his heart that someone had to save this massive beast, and so he did. And do you know what that deer did in return?"

"No." Benjamin hung on every word.

"When he was free, finally released from his captivity, instead of running away scared, he turned and thanked the young boy."

"He did?"

"A smile is the most powerful tool we are given. A smile and a wink, an adoring glance, can mean so much to one person. It tells that person, who may have been lost or alone, that he's loved. It shows you how we all have our gifts. That little boy felt the buck's appreciation and his heart swelled with happiness. Just moments earlier that little boy was sad. He was feeling lost and scared. After helping save a life, he walked away with a happy pride that only comes from doing good. This is what life is all about. One small act can mean so much. Just imagine what my Painting could be like if everyone did that."

"Your Painting sounds like a wonderful place, daddy. I so wish I could see it up close."

Gerald knew that his world was changing, though. Every minute that went by another fear was born. Every fear brought with it confusion and that confusion created disorder.

Soon, Gerald worried, his world would be unrecognizable. The people would need more than he could provide. They needed clarity and understanding. They needed to know the truth, but there was only one way...

Sure, Gerald tried. When they cried to him, he would send tears from the clouds. When there was joy, there was also sunlight. When someone asked for a sign, he would send a butterfly and when they asked for help, he'd will someone to be available.

Sometimes they listened, sometimes they didn't. Sometimes, unlikely people felt the message and found themselves at the right moment, able to help. It gave them clarity. Satisfaction. For some, it gave them humility. For others though - arrogance was born.

"I was called! I was chosen by the creator to help others. Look at what I can do. See with your own eyes the magic I have. Believe in me and know the truth of it all. Give me everything you have and become one of the selected to do Geody's will."

Oh, how Gerald hated that; singling people out; the weak and the vulnerable. They all had the power, they just didn't know it. If only someone could explain the truth to them.

As the years passed, Gerald watched and shared each individual tale with his son. Benjamin grew up with the world. He was being molded into a very important person because he was being taught lessons no other could truly impart. His story was just as important as each story he heard, because his story was being written as well.

"Dad, I want to go to your world. I want to set them straight."

"You can't just walk into my world, Son."

"Dad, if you've taught me anything growing up, you've taught me there is always a way. Where there is a will there's a way; as we all have the power to find it. One of these days I will find a way to go to these people and tell them what a wonderful father you are."

Gerald smiled at his son with an adoration as large as his heart could create. His smile was bright on the outside, but what the world was becoming was giving him pain on the inside.

When his son was old enough to understand, Gerald would share with him some of the more horrible details of his world - the things that he was ashamed of.

He knew his son needed to fully understand good before he could share with him the bad. He knew his son's heart was strong and his desire to do good would prevail. He knew his son would be able to change everything and he knew it would happen sooner than he would be ready for.

Chapter 5

"I don't believe!" The man stood at the top of the hilltop, screaming to the sky. "Show me your face! Prove to me you exist."

Gerald willed the clouds to roll in but then realized he was being goaded.

"Give me a sign or I will never believe. I demand you to show me something, anything."

He released his tension and a ray of sun peaked out from behind a cloud. Gerald took a deep breath, closed his eyes and willed the man's heart to change. The man paused for a moment and Gerald was hopeful that he had felt a twinge of love touch him... but the anger was stronger within him.

"The stories of the creator are impossible. Magic doesn't exist. This is all a fairytale meant to enchant young children."

Gerald wanted so badly to reach out and touch this man. To embrace him and show him 'I'm here.' He felt the man's words sting like a knife to the heart.

"There is nothing that can explain this, no one who can rationalize this story and truly accept these tales as fact. Anyone who claims they believe, must have some small bit of doubt within them, otherwise they would surely be considered crazy."

Was Gerald crazy? He created this world. He saved it. He watches over it still today and yet each day it made him more and more sad.

"Show me an adult who believes."

Gerald searched the world for anyone in the area to turn right and venture out towards this man. But the man continued screaming. "Show me someone who has never done wrong. Whose good nature is all there is to him. Show me someone who can prove you exist, who has seen you, known you."

The sadness built within Gerald. This man refused to believe without proof and yet Gerald could sense how powerfully he wanted to believe. This man was crying for vindication. He wanted so desperately to be wrong that every fiber of his being was screaming out for it.

"Send a messenger. Communicate your will to us. Tell us what you want, or we will never know."

A tear slipped down Gerald's cheek. His heart ached in his chest. He knew what he had to do – he had always known what he had to do. He had hoped he would have more time, more time to prepare, but he could feel that it was time. He had always known that the Painting would let him know when it was time.

Just then, from the opposite side of his world, Gerald heard a newborn baby cry out for the first time. Its wail pierced the hole growing in his heart. With every bit of love he had inside of him Gerald spoke to the man. "You will get your proof. Go tell the world, that soon, you will get your proof."

"Son!" Gerald called out from inside his den. "Son, would you come in here, please?"

"Yes Father." Benjamin walked into the room. He was nearing adulthood, and so full of love. He was as perfect as Gerald's intentions had ever been. He had been taught his entire life what he was meant to do – without truly knowing, and now it was time.

"Tell me what is in your heart, Son," he spoke, motioning to a chair and watching his son come in and stand by it.

Benjamin thought carefully, then spoke. "I have been filled with love - nothing but love from you and mom. I understand this life better than most. I have an insight that no one else could ever have for I have received the fundamental lessons of life through your world. I have seen passion through your eyes, an understanding and patience stronger than any mountain. I have felt your hopes, been a part of your dreams, and desire nothing more than to share your legend with others."

Gerald smiled sadly. "My Painting I will always treasure. But you, Son, you are my masterpiece. I have spent my lifetime perfecting the perfect. Teaching you, developing my message. Today I have been enlightened. I can now see further than I ever dreamed, and what I see is magnificent."

"Tell me, Father, what's happened?"

Gerald sighed. "Son, please sit down." There was a darkness building within him that he was almost afraid of. "Life is precious, here as well as in my world. Life begins and it ends but the point of it – is that it exists." Gerald formed his words carefully in his head before he spoke them. "You would be loved by two, adored by many and hated by all."

"How can that be?" Benjamin questioned but was stopped by his father's raised hand.

"Can you be strong?"

"Of course."

"Can you be brave?"

"I think so."

"Can you be patient?"

"Father?" Benjamin's head cocked to the side a bit and his eyebrows furled.

"Benjamin, there is still so much to learn. No one who has not lived the life could ever truly understand it all. You must be a part of it, to grow with it."

He gazed at his father, examining the sweat on his brow. He was puzzled by his father's face. It was filled with thrill and yet his eyes held terror. Gerald stared at him and yet Benjamin felt as if his father were looking through him, to the Painting that hung on the wall behind him.

"You would retain my love, you would always be my son, but you would be the son of another." A single tear caught the light of his desk lamp but then was blinked away. "Your memories would be there for you when you need them. My will would be a part of your soul. You will learn how to use it with time. You will learn everything you need to. You will KNOW everything."

He stood, then immediately fell to his knees in front of his son. He took Benjamin's hands within his, the tears were flowing freely.

"But Son, there is so much pain. More pain than you could possibly imagine. It's blinding. Its torture endures forever. I cannot do this to you without you knowing - without you understanding completely."

He cradled his son in his arms. He hugged him tightly. He was full-grown and the apple of his father's eye. A replica of perfection as only a father would ever see.

"You've said that you wanted to go. You've voiced your request; suggested it time and time again, but you weren't ready. Even knowing how, I would have hesitated because it would have meant letting you go.

But I know you are ready. I know it. I just need to hear it from you. You must say it. But think hard about this. This decision cannot be made lightly and it will last forever...." Gerald looked up into the quizzical eyes of his son, took a deep breath and asked, "Do you still want to go into my world?"

Benjamin turned and stared at the Painting on the wall. The universe was magnificent, the way it moved; the colors of space, the shooting stars, the rays of light. Then there was the world - the original Painting. From this distance the green and blues glistened in the night. It sparkled like a gemstone, reflecting a multitude of colors. He had NEVER seen it up close. He had always wondered what it was like inside of the Painting. It called to him.

He had spent his entire life dreaming about this moment. He had wanted to see his father's world since the very first bedtime story as he lay as an infant in his crib. He had worked hard, studied hard, and grown up with the willingness to do anything.

"Son, do you still want to visit my world?"

"Yes."

Chapter 6

"The Son is coming!"

Word of the creator's son spread across the land. The people rejoiced and the people rebelled. "Our creator is sending his son."

"Why?"

"To teach us. To rescue us."

"Rescue us from what?"

"Ourselves."

"I don't need rescuing."

"Everyone needs to be rescued."

Word spread like wildfires. It was impossible to understand and yet everyone knew. "He is coming."

People who believed, prepared. People who didn't believe, felt uncertainty. They didn't believe in the painter and yet, they feared the coming of his son. It was illogical to be afraid of something they didn't believe to be true, and yet their fears grew.

As some went about their days waiting with smiles and eager anticipation, others frowned and grumbled. They didn't know what to expect. They didn't want to be judged and they didn't want to be proven wrong.

The soon-to-be-parents were happily looking forward to the moment they would get to see their child, hold their newborn son in their arms and yet it wasn't *their* child. What would the creator's son be like? Would he look like them? Act like them? Talk like them? Would he grow up faster? Talk sooner? Walk quicker? Would he be as unique a phenomenon as the story of the painted world itself?

"Will he love us?"

"Of course he will." The soon-to-be mother sat down next to her husband, she held his hand. "Please don't be upset. Our love for him will be stronger, deeper than any other. He will be our baby. He will be raised by us. He will depend on us. He will be taught by us. He will grow up with his knowledge, but he will receive our values. What he will become will include what we teach him and if we do our job right..."

"He will love us as strong as any child who loves their parents." The husband kissed his wife on the forehead.

They were chosen. Why they were chosen of all of the couples in the entire world, they would never know. Were they the best choice? They couldn't be certain, but the creator, he was. The creator knew they were because they heard his call. They answered him.

"You will bring life to my Son. He will enter the painting through you and you will be responsible for raising him. You will teach him everything he needs to learn about your world. You will protect him until he is old enough to protect himself. He is my pride and joy. I will be watching over him. I will be watching over you all - as I always am."

Gerald walked into his son's room and noticed him standing outside of his closet staring in. The light was on, but he was just standing there.

"Son, is something wrong?"

"How do I pack for a trip like this?"

"You fill your heart to the top with all the love your mom and I can give."

Benjamin turned to look at his father. Gerald suddenly looked older. The worry lines were more visible. He smiled at his father, and then nodded.

"It is time."

Benjamin sat down on the side of his bed and exhaled. "Will it hurt?"

"No."

"How much time will pass by?"

"One day here is a year there. By the time you are seven a week will have passed. I imagine you will be gone for a little over a month."

"I will only live to be around 35?"

"You will live for as long as it takes for you to learn what you need to and teach what you are supposed to."

"What exactly is it that you want me to teach them?"

"You will know when the time is right. Once your message has been delivered, it will be the people who decide."

"What does that mean, Father?"

"You will figure it out, Son."

The mysteries of life were going to be a challenge to Benjamin, he knew, but he also looked forward to it. He hugged his mom goodbye, a long, drawn-out hug that would have to last for years. Then he lay down on the bed. Gerald kneeled down next to his son's bed side.

"Just close your eyes, Son. Breathe deeply and imagine my world; the Painting - the beauty within, the light, the sounds, the smells." Benjamin's breathing slowed – he was falling asleep. "Your journey will start in the dark, the unknown. You will understand but for a while, you will only be able to witness it. There will be much to learn, so much to discover. Your training will begin when the lights turn on."

Gerald had been holding his son's hand. He held it tight, as if he didn't want to let it go.

His arm trembled as did his quivering voice. He inhaled deeply, then slowly, Gerald let go of his son's hand and all fell away.

"You are now in the dark. It is peaceful. Serene. You feel warm inside, and you can hear the beating of a heart as you are filled with love from within.

Your journey will begin when the cold hits you for the first time. When the light blinds you; when the pain of the world fills you; when this happens - you will be born."

Chapter 7

As the bitter cold air struck his bare skin for the first time, Benjamin trembled. It was a shocking, harsh change from where he had been moments ago. His body filled with desperate, excruciating emotions that were screaming to be released.

As he exhaled a cry into the wintry night, he didn't recognize his voice. It was small and frail and filled with despair. He was a baby.

He felt himself being swaddled, wrapped in a blanket that felt rough against his soft new skin. The roughness made him cry more. The sound of his screaming pierced his delicate ears. The smells surrounding him were confusing and sharp. His eyes wouldn't open. He felt heavier. It was harder to breathe. The tears were flowing freely and his cries became louder. He was confused and lost. He was miserable!

But then he felt someone hold him - pulled deep into the arms of someone warm. She kissed his head, rocked him calmly, and held him tight. She embraced him tenderly and calmed him from within. His fears started to subside. He stopped crying. His breathing slowed. The quiet of the night filled his ears and the silence was beautiful.

Gerald heard his son being born and sobbed quietly, listening. He knew for a while his son would be fine. He would be taught, then he would learn, then he would educate others. It would be good for quite a while. He rested on his recliner with his head back and his eyes closed, comforted in this knowledge.

It would be a long, long month - but the reason would be worth it. His purpose would be seen by everyone and it would be good. He knew this - HE KNEW - but still a part of his heart, the deepest darkest part of his heart, ached. There was a twinge of grief that was clawing at his soul and he had a feeling, this anguish would overwhelm him as the time neared. He feared it.

As the morning sun rose over the hills, Benjamin opened his eyes and took in its beauty. The rays of light illuminated the world in a way that nothing else ever could. The sky sparkled and glowed with a thousand similar colors. Red and violet, yellow and orange all combined to resemble a pallet, being mixed and blended to create the perfect color before the first paint stroke on a canvas of a brand-new day.

Yet the canvas was already painted. The hills of green transformed from dark to light. The grasses were various heights and colors. There was no way to count the number of greens that were used to paint a single blade and yet each piece of grass blended to form a hillside.

The trees and plants, displayed a depth of texture and color that was unlike any he had ever seen. As the light hit them, it showcased leaves of varying sizes, assorted shades of greens. It was almost overwhelming the detail that was put into every smudge.

The effect of seeing this beauty for the first time was overpowering. Benjamin stared at it until his eyes hurt, until the tears began to flow. Without being able to articulate the beauty he was taking in, all he could do was let the emotions out.

The cry woke Gerald. He looked into the painting and watched as his son was picked up for the first time this morning and cared for as any child would be, should be. He smiled brightly, a tear forming in the corner of his eye as a call pulled his attention elsewhere.

By the end of the day Gerald looked back in on the progress of his son. He had just pulled himself to his feet. His tiny unsteady legs trembled under the weight of his one-year-old body, but he did it - he was standing. His parents watched with proud smiles, holding each other when they saw his mouth open. They waited with excited anticipation as he inhaled – focusing on what he needed to do.

Watching, waiting, excited and expectant, Gerald listened as Benjamin looked up and closed his tiny eyes and then spoke his first ever words... "da da"

Each year, as Benjamin grew, so did his understanding of this world. He learned how to walk and talk, sing and dance. He played, made friends, went to school and read.

This world was full of unknown possibilities; the stories, the songs, the plays. The creativity inside each and every person was astounding. Each person was born with so much possibility. There was so much opportunity. The fact that they could become anything their heart desires astounded Benjamin.

His father had created the perfect world, so full of life with so many options. A single choice could open the door to an array of potential. They couldn't see it - not really, but they had so many opportunities to follow their dreams, their hearts desires, and so few of them did just that.

A young boy swung a bat at a ball and missed. He swung it with all of his might. If he would have hit that ball, he would have made a home run - all he needed was practice. But he gave up. He cried because he missed, threw the bat to the ground and gave up.

Benjamin saw how close he had come, he could see the fork in the road before this young boy. If he would have stood there and tried again, the next pitch would have been hit. He would have knocked it out of the park and started himself along the path of a great baseball player, but he threw it away.

As he sat in the crowd, contemplating what the boy had thrown away, he watched as the next opportunity came walking up to him. The coach's older son kneeled down in front of the boy. His arm was in a sling and even though he was only a teenager, his face held the wisdom of an adult.

He spoke to the boy. He showed him his shoulder, and explained how he had been following his dream of becoming a pro ball player, until he threw his shoulder out.

Benjamin saw how the boy listened, wiped a tear from his cheek and sat up a bit straighter in the dugout. He nodded and smiled and then stood up. He walked back out to the plate and picked up his bat. As he awaited the pitch, Benjamin returned his gaze to the coach's son who was watching and he saw his father's hand pat the teens back and then disappear. He knew this was his father giving him an "atta boy" and this made him feel very good inside.

Benjamin knew his father had opened another door for that young boy, and it was the coach's son who answered. As he heard the crack of the bat hit the ball, Benjamin returned his attention to the young boy who stood there in awe watching the ball fly farther and farther away. Everyone in the crowd stood and cheered and yelled at him to "Run! Run!"

The boy dropped the bat to the ground and began running to first base as quick as his little legs could take him. The smile that spread across his face was as big as his own father's smile as he watched from afar.

While this wasn't the first time Benjamin had witnessed his father's work here, it was one of the first times he saw his father truly intervene and suddenly, he understood.

Benjamin knew well how his father would watch over the Painting. He had witnessed his emotions skip around from happy to sad from angry to glad. He could easily be laughing and crying at the same time.

It always made him wonder, especially with the understanding of how time works here, how he could possibly hear and be a part of everybody's lives at every minute of every day, even when he slept.

But then Benjamin would witness his father sending love - so much love. A huge flowing wave of caring and hope would sweep into the Painting and blanket everything inside of it like a thick heavy coat of paint. He was sending the will and the way. He was giving everybody the chance to be the solution, to answer his call and help others by just listening and feeling. It was all about doing good deeds.

It excited Benjamin to learn how easy it was to do his father's work here. He gave everyone exactly what they needed to answer anyone's call at any time. Benjamin understood. He realized the simplicity of this complex situation and he valued that knowledge. The dilemma posed before him, was how to teach everyone else.

Chapter 8

As Benjamin grew up, he continued learning. With his mouth closed and his eyes and heart open, he witnessed the beauty of his father's plan in just about everything he looked at. Every person, plant and animal, every action, deed or phrase, gave an opportunity to be a part of a greater plan.

The problem he kept seeing was when someone turned the corner, many didn't follow through. He could sense that they felt it - even if it was just for a fraction of a second. They were given a decision: answer, or walk away. It was their decision as to what they would do.

Sometimes they would see someone who needed help and while their heartstrings tugged at the person to help, their brain reminded them they were running late. Maybe they saw danger, maybe they saw no need to help, maybe they thought someone else will do it – so why should they?

Yet as Benjamin continued to observe, he'd see that maybe it was the next person that came along that answered the call, or maybe the third. His father had answered that person's plea by providing not one, but many opportunities. Sometimes it took more than one. Sometimes, the potential would keep going down the line until it found the right person. Sometimes, the line was so long that the person awaiting an answer – gave up.

When Benjamin was about ten years old, he began sharing what he had been learning.

Not as eloquently as he had wanted since his education on this planet was still in progress, but he was teaching his peers what he could.

"I am the painter's son. My father was the artist who painted this world."

While many joshed and laughed at the idea, some wanted to believe and others absolutely did. The ones that didn't believe didn't care to hear more. The ones that weren't sure if they could believe, well they asked for proof or watched from afar.

"I heard stories that the creator was sending his son but it was such a long time ago."

"I was born into this world. I was a baby. I had to grow up, just like you."

"How do you know YOU are the one they were talking about?"

"I just know. I was born knowing. I've seen my father at work here. I've heard him speak to me."

It took them a while to accept; the others who did, helped. But it was his lessons that validated his claims.

One afternoon three of his friends joined Benjamin for a walk. They walked out to a nearby pasture and gazed out at the field.

"What do you see?" Benjamin inquired.

"A field," Jacob spoke quick.

"A tree," Max added.

Benjamin smiled. "Tell me about that tree."

"It's a tree, what's there to tell?" Danny asked obviously confused as to the purpose of this talk.

Jacob described the tree. "Green leaves. Brown trunk."

"What else? Tell me about the importance of this tree." Benjamin looked at Jacob as they started to walk towards it.

Jacob shrugged his shoulders, so Benjamin began to describe the tree himself.

"That tree stands alone in this field. Its massive size towers over the grass. Its limbs stretch out so far, they almost bend down to the ground in search for rest. Its very existence reflects a bold symbol of solidarity - that anyone who stands up for their beliefs will prevail."

As they neared the tree, Benjamin started pointing out the details.

"The leaves are made up of many shades of green. Each leaf differs slightly from the next, from its color, to its shape. Some are small, some are large, some have been chewed on by bugs or torn by birds flying by. They are a lighter color green on the underside and darker on the top. They have veins that feather out, getting smaller towards the ends."

The boys looked closely at the leaves as Benjamin redirected his attention to the tree's trunk. "The bark is coarse and textured. The trunk is not necessarily brown, but shades of brown and grey. Because of the texture, there is dimension; flat rough areas and deep cavernous gaps. Those crevasses provide pathways for ants and bugs to crawl up." The boys directed their attention to the bark and Danny poked at the ants. Benjamin continued.

"This tree provides shade for us. It's cooler under here than it was out there in the field."

"I'm thankful for that," Max spoke.

"This tree also provides shelter. It is a home for the animals. That squirrel has created a nest in the upper branches. That family of birds have built their nest in the lower branches. That woodpecker has drilled a hole for its home in the trunk."

The children looked and noticed all of the different homes that existed within the tree's limbs. Benjamin continued.

"Over here you can even see where a buck scraped his antlers against the lower limbs." Jacob rubbed his finger along the smoothly rubbed area.

"This tree produces acorns, which the squirrels and birds eat. It provides areas for the squirrels to store food for the winter. This tree does so much for so many."

"I never thought about it that way," Jacob spoke quietly.

"Guess trees are pretty important," Max declared. The boys took all of that in.

"But that's not all," Benjamin spoke. "We climb their branches and get exercise. When we look out over the canopy, we can see the world in a completely different way. We are taller and can look down at the world. We can see more, can expand our awareness."

"Wow," Jacob spoke, looking up at the light shining in through the leaves.

"Look, someone carved their initials into the trunk," Max added, starting to notice details.

"Good job." Benjamin smiled, "The tree is a way for someone to declare their love for someone else."

"I know of a girl who comes out here to read all of the time. She enjoys the quiet and the cool shade as she leans back against the tree trunk," Danny offered. Benjamin smiled and nodded.

"When I was younger, we used to hang a swing from the branches of a tree and it provided hours worth of entertainment."

"Oh yeah, we once had a tree next to a river and we hung a rope from it and swung out over the water and dropped in."

"The twigs that fall are collected to build campfires for keeping warm." Jacob added. "And woodworkers build furniture and tools."

"See," Benjamin smiled, "there is a lot to this tree. But there is even more than that."

He pointed to the roots as they stretched across the ground spanning up over and around the rocks. "These roots have had to work hard to grow. They're journey has been fraught with obstacles. Large rocks have blocked their pathway. They had to adapt and change in order to keep growing. What's important about that is that they need to be as wide as the widest branch to support its growth. This is very important - without a strong foundation the rest of the tree will topple over. If the roots would have stopped at the first obstacle, the growth of this massive tree would have been stunted. It never would have grown as tall and wide as it has. It would have been unable to give us shade, provide them shelter and supply us food."

Everybody sat down around the tree and thought about that for a few moments. "Obstacles are placed in our lives to help us grow, to become stronger." It was an insightful thing for a young boy to say.

A light breeze cooled the sweat from their brows, and Benjamin then asked another question. "Will this tree look the same in a couple months?"

Everyone thought about that and then Max answered. "No! Soon its leaves will turn red and orange and fall to the ground."

"I love jumping in piles of fall leaves."

"Me too!"

"What about a month after that? What will the tree look like then?"

"The leaves will be gone; it'll be bare."

"Right. It marks the seasons: fall and winter. A tree tells us time. It also mimics the stages of our life. We live in seasons and one season we will lose our leaves and leave nothing but a shell. However, the next season we will be reborn and become new. "

"Reborn anew?" Danny questioned but didn't think anyone heard.

"And did you know that the leaves of this tree generate oxygen? The air we breathe comes from the trees and plants around us."

Benjamin waited for all of that to sink in before he spoke again. "So what do you see here now? Just a tree?"

"No, there's so much more."

"And *that* is Father's design. Everything has been painstakingly painted for a reason. Everything has a purpose, multiple purposes. Every single thing in the Painting has THAT kind of detail and purpose – including us. It's when we slow down, take a long look at what's in front of us, that we begin to see."

Chapter 9

As the four boys rested, they watched a couple other children enter the field throwing a ball back and forth. They watched for a while, until Jacob stood up and began looking around the tree. He wanted to refocus his attention on the masterpiece before him when he noticed something that seemed to confuse him.

"Benjamin, what about this?"

Benjamin, Max and Jacob all stood and walked around to the opposite side of the tree. There they saw a burnt limb that had been split down the middle and sat dead on the ground.

"Can you explain this?"

"It was struck by lightning," Max spoke, certain as to what had happened.

"Right, but why would your father strike down and kill a part of a tree that has so much symbolism, importance and meaning?"

"Yeah?" Max and Danny spoke in unison.

Benjamin smiled. "Look closer. Look inside that burnt out crevice and see what's inside." Max leaned in and saw a colony of milky white worm-looking things crawling around.

"What are they?"

Jacob took a peek. "Termites."

"They are eating the wood. This tree limb is providing sustenance," Benjamin offered.

"Yeah, but when it's gone, they'll move on to this amazing tree."

"If they do?"

"They'll kill it. We can't let that happen," Jacob voiced his concern.

"We don't have to. It is our will to do something about it."

Max tilted his head curiously. "What do you mean Benjamin?"

With a smile, "You've seen a problem and my father has given you the will and ability to do something about that problem. It is up to you to decide whether you are going to listen. Will you ignore the problem and let the termites live another day to eat this tree? Will you kill the termites, solving the problem but ending a civilization? Will you move the tree limb to another part of the field, so they can live?"

"I choose the latter," Danny spoke.

"Why?"

"Because," Danny grinned "it sounds like the right thing to do."

"What if the termites venture back over here?" Benjamin suggested.

"What?" Danny spoke, confused. He had been certain that his answer was the right one.

"What if you move the termites over there and they finish off the dead tree limb, then come back over here later and start in on the tree?"

"So we should kill the termites now?" Max spoke ready to start stomping on them.

Benjamin stopped him. "I'm not saying you should kill them, and I'm not saying you shouldn't. What I'm asking, is for you to follow the pathway that has already been set. Danny has already decided to move the limb. Consider the fact that the task is done, the limb has been moved, the termites have eaten it and are ready to move on. What happens next?"

Jacob sat up. "Well I know that Danny moved the limb, maybe now I go and check on the termites to see what they're doing."

"Good. But what if two days from now you've forgotten about the termites?"

"Then I'll go," Max added.

"That's my father at work. That's how simple and hard life is." Benjamin sat up. He looked up at a distant storm cloud rolling in. We could decide to do something, we could decide not to do something, or that storm cloud could bring with it rain that may wash the termites away and the tree will still be safe."

Now I'm starting to get confused again," Jacob admitted.

Benjamin realized he may have been throwing too much at his friends at once but he had already begun. "Jacob could move the termites. Max could stomp on them, or those boys playing ball in the field out there could pick up this stick and bring it home not even knowing about the termites.

The termites may be washed away from the tree by the coming rains or the storm may bring another bolt of lightning to strike another tree limb down to continue feeding them. Each day, each moment brings with it an unlimited amount of possibilities. Everyone and everything in this world has the opportunity to bring change. Each prospect of modifying the world brings with it more chances and variations.

The possibilities to do good are endless, as is the odds of doing something bad. It's how we deal with those actions that define who we are and how we will grow."

Benjamin looked at his three friends who were staring at him with their mouths open.

"Too much?" He asked.

The three nodded in unison.

"Sorry." Benjamin sat there letting his friends take all of that in.

Danny looked out over the field to the other kids playing. "Nobody else thinks about things the way you do, Benjamin." The others followed his gaze to the field. The three of them, and the kids playing in the field, were all the same age, but suddenly Jacob, Danny and Max felt older and wiser.

"It almost doesn't seem fair – knowing as much as you do. Having all of this awareness..." Jacob trailed off.

Benjamin looked at him curiously. He could sense Jacob's thought process was almost overwhelmed. He finally turned to Benjamin and asked, "Can you ever just be a child?"

"What do you mean?"

"I've never seen you just go out there and play. You're always sitting somewhere watching others."

"He's played before," Max offered, "I saw him throw a ball up in the air and catch it."

Jacob nodded, "But were you just playing for fun, or were you looking at the ball, judging the speed it was going to fall, testing the wind, feeling the leather wrapped around it?"

"What do you think?" Benjamin asked with a smile.

"I think you know more about that baseball than I can possibly fathom. I think you know more about it than a pro-ball player could understand."

"And?" Benjamin was curious where Jacob was going with this.

"And, I think it's sad that you know as much as you do. You can't just be a child and have fun and live with no worries or responsibilities for just a while. My father is always telling me to stop worrying, that my job is to be a kid because this is the only time we get. But Benjamin, you don't get even this time, do you?"

The look on Benjamin's face changed. His eyes lowered and his brow furled. He knew he was different, but it had never been put so bluntly before.

"Don't you listen to him," Max interrupted. "I think the fact that you know so much is exhilarating. Imagine all of the things you can do with what you know."

"But he just said that he can't control it, everyone has the ability to do whatever they want. He can't change anything no matter what he says or does."

"That's not what he said, he said his father will make sure what needs to happen, happens."

"No, his father can only watch and hope for the best. Bad things happen. That's why he's here. To teach us. Right?" Danny asked noticing how conflicted Benjamin was looking.

"I think everything you all are saying is interesting. I'm trying to teach you about my father's world and you are looking out for me. You are worried about my well-being and I appreciate that."

The four of them looked out at the others playing when they all heard a loud thunder clap. It made them shudder as the other boys took off running towards home.

"Guess they've got the right idea. Apparently, this tree is prone to lightning strikes." Max stood and stretched.

"Good point," Danny added as he scrambled to his feet. The two of them helped Jacob and Benjamin off the ground and they began walking home.

As they walked away from the tree, Jacob looked back at it. He saw the storm clouds rolling in and it made him shiver. Thinking about everything they had just learned and the knowledge Benjamin had instilled, was still spiraling around in his head.

He knew he would never look at another tree the same way again and he began to wonder what else Benjamin would teach them that would change the way they saw the world?

Chapter 10

Sitting in class listening to the teacher describe today's assignment, Benjamin began to wonder what his father would teach him about the Painting today. He looked out the window and noticed the clouds drifting by in the sky. He noticed how they would at times block the sun's light, but then as they moved and parted, bright rays of light would beam through the openings and shine down on the world. It was as if his father was putting a spotlight on small patches of land. Benjamin sat up straight and craned his neck to see where the light was pointing and saw a pond shimmering off in the distance.

The way the water moved with the wind made the sunlight refracting off of it look like glitter. With imagination combined with what he could see, Benjamin found himself standing along the shoreline. He watched ducks swimming across the water. He witnessed turtles ducking under the water after a quick breath of air and then he heard birds singing in nearby trees.

Benjamin realized he had let his mind wonder completely out of the classroom. He hadn't heard the teacher and wasn't even worried about it until a loud alarm rang out. Not knowing what was going on, he returned his attention to the class and the teacher announcing this was a fire drill. The teacher instructed the students to line up single file and walk out of the school building.

The alarm was deafening. It hurt Benjamin's ears and he began to wonder quietly what the animals and birds felt when they heard this loud, high-pitched squawk. He could cover his ears with his hands, they couldn't.

Standing outside, even amongst the commotion of the students, teachers and reverberation of the alarm, Benjamin felt happy. He always found himself most comfortable within the natural world his father painted. After a while, the okay came to reenter the school, and the students began to walk back to the building. As they neared, Benjamin heard a loud thump. The sound attracted everyone's attention and many of the startled students began to vocally express their shock over the scene unfolding before them. Just a few feet in front of Benjamin was a bird lying motionless on the ground. He stepped up to the bird, kneeled down and picked it up.

"Is it dead?" One of the children asked.

"What happened?" Came another inquiry.

Benjamin held the bird's lifeless body in the palm of his hand and cupped his other hand over it. The pain he felt in his heart for this poor little bird grew. It was the alarm that interfered with his flight. His direction was obstructed by the sound. It was their fault for this small bird's collision and he felt so strongly about fixing the situation; he willed the bird to get better. He wanted so much for this bird to shake it off, stretch his wings out and lift off of his hands and fly away, that at that moment, he believed it would happen.

With eyes closed, and a tear streaking down his face, he opened his hands. That's when he felt the bird press its feet against his palm and leap into the sky. Benjamin heard everyone gasp in amazement as they watched the bird fly away. When he opened his eyes and saw the bird flying higher, higher up, he smiled and whispered a thank you to his father.

As he rose back to his feet, he felt his father speak to him. "That was all you, Son. You are a part of me, and thus you have the power."

Moments later in the hallway Danny and Jacob came running up to Benjamin. "Someone said you brought a bird back to life."

Benjamin said nothing.

"Another moment later Max came running up, "Hey, I heard you were taking credit for bringing a bird back to life, but it had just been stunned."

Jacob turned to Max. "The bird was dead, he saved it."

"Were you there? Did you see it?"

"No, I don't need to, I believe Benjamin."

"Believe him?" Danny interjected, "He hasn't said a word."

"Sure he did. He saved the bird's life."

"No he didn't." Danny spoke matter-of-factly. The three looked at Benjamin, who stood there looking back with his mouth shut.

"The bird had been stunned and you woke it. Right?" Max asked.

"The bird was dead and you saved it. Right?" Jacob countered.

"Benjamin, tell us what happened," Danny begged, not wanting to jump to conclusions.

Benjamin looked at them sadly. "Something happened with the bird. People know what they saw. They said what they saw and they all saw something different. The only person who asked to know the truth was Danny - and you only asked because the confusion has made you uneasy."

"So which is it?" Jacob asked. "Was the bird dead or stunned?"

"Does it matter?" Benjamin countered.

The three looked at each other then back to Benjamin. "Of course it matters."

"You could have done a miracle!"

"Would you only respect me if I had?"

"No," they replied

"Would you think less of me if the bird had been stunned and I comforted it until it was able to fly away?"

"Of course not."

"Is that what happened?" Max asked.

"I can't tell you what happened," he admitted. *Benjamin didn't know what happened, not really.* And within minutes of him having done whatever it was, he had two conflicting stories floating around.

"Liar," A tall girl spoke, as she walked by Benjamin with a glare on her face.

Danny was shocked. "What did you lie about?" He looked at Benjamin with worry.

"I haven't said a word," Benjamin admitted. "I can no more control their thoughts as you can. They are free to take what they saw or hear and form their own opinions. It is the way of this world, and all I can do is be me--who my father made me to be."

"Yeah, but did you?" Danny asked again.

Jacob tagged him on the shoulder, "Dude! It doesn't matter!" He spoke, with exasperation.

"Can you show us some magic?" Two girls ran up to Benjamin. They were star struck with the idea that he had saved the bird's life and wanted to see more for themselves.

"Doesn't it?" Danny looked back at Jacob, who was just as lost.

The three boys realized the truth of what Benjamin had said, through the actions of his deed and what hadn't been said. Their hearts hurt for Benjamin as the various looks of thrill, anger, fear and confusion turned towards him.

Benjamin seemed to know that this uncertainty, the misunderstandings of others, was going to be a new constant in his life. The perplexity of his goal within this Painting was going to cause turmoil and chaos and it would carry through for the rest of his life.

This must have been why his father had looked so worried that day. He knew what was going to happen and there was no way to prepare his son for it. It just had to happen.

Chapter 11

As the years progressed, so did Benjamin's studies. With an opportunity to take an elective, he chose art, and this is when he was able to realize his true gift. He learned about a way to revolutionize the way he delivered his message.

Learning how to draw and paint helped to enhance Benjamin's expressive abilities. As situations between friends or strangers arose, his keen insights as to what could be, inspired the desire to doodle. He began drawing scenes, not the way they were, but how he saw they *could be*. It was when he shared those scenes that he began enacting change - change for the better. His capabilities were growing as he followed the footsteps of his father.

One morning, while sitting on a bench in town, Benjamin watched the people as they went along the pathway of their day. As he found himself staring at them, taking in the details of their lives, he was also sketching.

A young girl walking hand in hand with her grandmother caught Benjamin's attention. She looked so bored as she shuffled her feet. As they walked down the sidewalk, the young girl stared longingly at the clothes in the storeroom windows. As they walked past Benjamin, he ripped a page out of his notebook and handed it to her. She didn't look at it at that moment. Her grandmother was pulling her along and she needed to keep up.

Hours later she sat in the back of a room listening to sewing machines buzzing away. Her grandmothers quilting class was busy creating a new quilt design when one of the ladies walked up to her. She looked at the paper lying next to the girl on the table and spoke.

"That's a beautiful sketch, why don't you see what you can do with some of these scraps of material?"

The young girl looked up at the lady inquisitively then down at the paper Benjamin had given her. She stared at it for the longest moment, and then glanced over to the pile of material. Suddenly a creative spark ignited within her. She took a piece of the colored cloth in her hand and draped it over her doll. Then she grabbed another piece and wrapped it around the doll's hips.

"What a beautiful dress you've started," another lady spoke as she walked by.

Suddenly, the little girl realized how important this day was going to be. While she had hated the idea of spending her afternoon here with her grandmother's old friends, this opportunity helped her realize a dream. She loved fashion and design. She loved clothes and this was an opportunity to start designing her own clothes.

If Benjamin hadn't been there this morning, if he hadn't handed her that sheet of paper, if her grandmother's friend hadn't noticed, she may have let this day go by without realizing her desires. How easy it would have been to continue to sit here moping. Bored. Focused on the negative instead of making the best out of the opportunity ahead of her.

That afternoon as she and her grand-mother walked back the other way across town, she saw Benjamin sitting on the bench. She ran up to him and showed him her doll's new dress. "I made this today because of what you drew. Thank you!"

Benjamin understood and smiled. This young girl was one of many lives Benjamin changed with his doodles today alone. He started being more adamant about his sketches. He'd finish them as quickly as he could so he could share them with those who inspired them. Before long, Benjamin found that people were searching for him, lining up to receive a sketch of what their future was going to be like. Of course, it didn't really work that way, but how could Benjamin explain that if he couldn't explain how he had this ability.

Some doodles never got ripped out of his sketchpad and shared. He wondered if they would ever have a chance to change lives or if these were missed opportunities. He began wishing he knew more people so he could find the intended recipients of these drawings. Maybe he should start traveling?

Sammy and Franklin were known as the town's biggest troublemakers. Sammy loved to incite anger and cause problems.

He'd key cars, graffiti storefronts, break windows, and steal from local establishments. While no one really knew it was him causing all of the trouble because he was never caught, they all had their ideas.

Franklin never really wanted to do these things, but he joined Sammy because he was his friend. He was also slightly afraid *not* to do it.

Tonight, as they kicked cans around a back-alley way, Sammy got another wicked smile on his face. He looked at Franklin with this wry, evil look and then glanced at a rather large window.

"Ah, you don't want to do that, do you?" Franklin began, hoping he could talk his friend out of more vandalism.

"Want to? I have to! That guy kicked me out of his store today for no apparent reason."

"You've stolen from him many times in the past," Franklin reprimanded.

"Yeah, but he doesn't know that."

"But, what if..."

"What if what?" Sammy countered the hunched-over Franklin, trying desperately to find a way to get his friend to stop misbehaving. "What if I just let them mistreat me, us? What if I just sit back and let these people walk all over us? What kind of friend would I be if I didn't look out after you?"

"But they didn't kick *me* out," Franklin offered, trying to help.

"So it's okay they kicked *me* out?" Sammy growled angrily. "It's okay they mistreat me so long as they don't mistreat you?"

"No. No it's not okay," Franklin sighed and acknowledged reluctantly.

"Are you sticking up for them? Are they your new friends?"

"No, Sammy, they're not."

"Then why don't you do the honors?" Sammy smirked as he kicked the can over towards Franklin's feet.

Franklin looked at the can.

"Do it," Sammy insisted. He watched Franklin look at the can and hesitate. The anger was building within him.

It was dusk, Benjamin had drawn all day. His sketch pad was almost empty. The only pages left were doodles that he didn't finish in time to hand out. He was walking home alone when he heard the sound of glass shattering off in the distance. He stopped and turned to face the sound, curious as to what had happened when he saw two boys racing around the corner laughing.

As they ran towards Benjamin, Sammy closed in and when he was within distance, he knocked Benjamin's sketchbook out of his hands. As the book slammed to the ground and flipped open, Benjamin watched as Sammy continued running, laughing hysterically.

Franklin, however, felt a twinge of guilt. He didn't run as fast as Sammy so he was trailing behind at quite a distance. He was also slightly overweight and already out of breath. When he saw Benjamin turn back and look at Sammy, Franklin slowed to a stop.

For some reason he stopped directly in front of Benjamin. Their eyes caught. The two of them faced each other, and Franklin didn't know why. It was awkward, and yet, calming. He was able to catch his breath and as he exhaled, he saw Benjamin's eyes glace down to his sketch-book.

When Franklin realized Benjamin was starting to bend down to get his book he spoke, "Wait, let me get that for you." He quickly squatted down and picked the book up into his hands. It was open and as he stood back up, he glanced at the picture the book had opened to.

It was a picture of someone handing another person a book. He stared at the picture a bit longer. It was dark. There was pencil shading all around the two figures, as if it took place near nighttime. But then Franklin recognized the figures in the book. This was a sketch of him, handing the book to Benjamin - exactly as he was doing now.

With a pang of reluctance, he did exactly as the sketch had shown. He handed the book to Benjamin, who took it. He watched as Benjamin glanced down at the picture and then back up at Franklin. He then ripped the page from the sketchbook, and handed it to the boy.

"You have a good night," Benjamin spoke as he walked away.

Franklin stood there, dumbfounded for a few moments, until he finally glanced back down at the paper in his hand. When he saw the pencil sketch of the act that he had just done--a sketch that had been drawn much earlier in the day and long before he had ever dreamed of running down this street--he cried.

Franklin had only heard stories about the Painter's son. He had never met him... until tonight.

Chapter 12

Franklin stood there alone on the sidewalk for the longest time. The knowledge of what had just taken place was spiraling around in his head. He felt as if his eyes had been opened and he was seeing clearly, as if the light was brighter than the night sky.

"I thought I lost you!" Sammy yelled down the street when he saw Franklin from afar.

Snapping out of his daze, Franklin looked at Sammy strolling towards him and quickly folded the drawing in his palms and tucked it into his back pocket.

"Where did you go? I thought you were right behind me."

Franklin shrugged, knowing better than mentioning any of this to his friend. Sammy was the only person in town who seemed to give any notice to Franklin. Being slightly chubby and quite too shy to start his own conversations, Franklin had always been alone.

When Sammy found Franklin, way back when, he had attempted to cause trouble and pick on him. But when Franklin stood up and his heft and weight towered over the boy, Sammy instead, became quite scared.

He almost backed away, but with a need to keep his tough-guy routine, he half-laughed and joked it off. With Sammy chuckling about the situation, Franklin didn't realize how afraid he looked. Without much knowledge of social interactions, he believed Sammy's laugh was an attempt at camaraderie and misconstrued it as friendship.

Franklin really liked having someone to hang out with and talk to, albeit he didn't do much talking. He did do a lot of listening. Sammy, on the other hand, really liked the idea of having this large guy being near him. It made him look even tougher. He became aware that they would make a good team. Sammy could do whatever he wanted, and no one would be able to stop him for fear of being pummeled. It seemed like a perfect match.

"I'm glad I found you, I thought you got picked up by the cops."

"You were worried about me?" Franklin smiled adoringly at his friend.

Sammy frowned, "No, of course not. It's just more fun to make trouble with someone else around."

As the two of them walked off, Sammy told Franklin everything that had entered his mind since shattering the glass window, and when he was done with that, he began talking about their next caper and what he was thinking they would do next.

It was a long night. They finally settled down in their favorite hangout, an abandoned garage just outside of town. Franklin was grateful for the rest and, when he leaned back in a chair and stretched out his legs and feet, he exhaled as if he had walked miles.

"You should really get in shape, Sammy spoke with the intention of pointing out how much larger Franklin had gotten since they met.

"And you care about my health."

Sammy's brow furled, "It's not easy to break in new friends."

"It's cool that you care," Franklin smiled, not catching the sarcasm that was rolling off of Sammy's tongue.

Franklin shifted in his chair and felt the crunch of the folded paper in his back pocket. He rolled to his side with two attempts and yanked the wad out. He unfolded it and looked at it again. He began to remember how unique that moment felt, how light and simple the world seemed at that moment. He was lost in thought about that, when Sammy snatched the paper from his hand.

"What's this?" Sammy spoke as he peered at the drawing.

"Nothing."

"Nothing? It looks like you."

"I think it is me."

"You think?"

"I think that was Benjamin, the Painter's son who you passed and smacked his book from his hands. I stopped and picked up his book and when I handed it back to him, he gave me this."

Sammy was stunned and yet felt an agitation build within him. "Why would you pick up his book for him?"

"It felt like the right thing to do."

"When do we *ever* do the right thing?"

Franklin shrugged his shoulders.

Sammy looked at the paper again, and a shiver went down his spine. A moment later he crumpled it into a ball in his hand and tossed it over his shoulder. "It's just a stupid drawing. You're just too good for your own good."

"But don't you think that looked like me? How do you think he drew that moment before it happened?"

"It's all part of the scam, Franklin. That's why I'm here; to make sure you don't get manipulated."

"But..."

"Forget about it. I'm your friend. I'm the one who looks out after you."

"I know you are," Franklin agreed quickly realizing Sammy was getting angry. He didn't like it when Sammy got mad. He would say and do very mean things and so Franklin always went out of his way to keep those moments from happening.

Chapter 13

It had been nearly a week since that chance encounter on the sidewalk where Benjamin handed Franklin the sketch that opened his eyes.

Franklin was terrified of upsetting Sammy by talking about it, but ever since that night, Franklin couldn't get it out of his head. He wanted to do something more with his life. It wasn't until this afternoon, while Sammy was preoccupied with another group, that Franklin found himself walking through the park and spotted Benjamin on a bench sketching. He approached.

"What are you working on?"

"Just doodling."

"Who is that?" Franklin asked pointing to the drawing.

Benjamin glanced at it and then up to Franklin and smirked, "I don't know."

"What do you mean you don't know? I thought you knew everything."

"Sometimes scenes and pictures of people come to me and I sketch them as I see them. They weren't brought on by someone as they walked past me, they were just there."

"Does that happen a lot?"

"Kind of."

"And you sketch them all?"

"I try. There's a reason I see them."

"But if you don't know who the sketches are of, how will you get them to the people who need to see them?"

Benjamin looked at Franklin, a smile spread across his face. "Maybe that's why you are here."

"Me?"

"Maybe you are meant to find these people and deliver my pictures to them."

"But I can't..."

"What? You can't walk? You can't see the faces of the people who are out and about in town? You can't recognize their facial features and walk up and hand them something without saying a word or even so much as interrupting their path?"

"Well, I can do that, I just... I thought you would do it."

"I'm in charge of drawing, maybe you're in charge of delivering those drawings. Maybe it's my father's plan."

"You don't know if it's the plan?"

"There are many plans, Franklin. Many opportunities within this life. Each pathway that falls before you has an alternate road. It's up to you to choose the route you want to take."

"What if I choose a different road?"

"That is your will. It is one of the many gifts my father has bestowed upon you."

"Even if I don't do what he wants me to?"

"My father wants you to be happy. That is all. He painted for you a world of beauty and perfection and he gave you the choice to experience it in any way you desire."

"Wow," Franklin spoke as his thoughts swirled within his head.

Benjamin returned to his sketchpad. He put the final touches on his picture and then closed his book. He then handed it to Franklin.

"What are you doing?"

"Giving you my sketchpad."

"Why?"

"So you can deliver my pictures to the people who need them."

"I never said I was going to do it."

"You didn't need to. It is now yours. You can do with it what you want."

"What if I throw it away?"

"That's your choice."

"But you put a lot of hard work into it. Wouldn't you be upset?"

"I couldn't be upset at you for doing whatever you want with your book."

"But it's yours."

"Not anymore. I gave it to you." Benjamin stood from the bench. "Have fun, Franklin. Enjoy your life. Fill it with moments that you can look back on and smile about."

Over the course of many years, Benjamin received the rewards of his wish; to be able to share his sketches and message with more people. He began traveling, walking along the country side, visiting town after town.

Word spread across the glossy canvas of this world. The Painter's son was telling futures, performing enchantments and sharing insights about their planet. Many people liked it and sought him out. Many didn't. Those that wanted to learn more, who wanted to meet the son of the Painter, traveled long distances to find him.

Benjamin's closest friends had to get creative so as to find some quiet time and a safe place for Benjamin to rest. He was almost always surrounded by crowds. It took a lot out of him. He longed for the days he could sit around and not have nearly as many demands expected of him, and yet, he was always energized when he was able to share his father's plan with huge crowds.

One day, as Benjamin rose to the sound of singing birds and a bright sunny day, he announced to his friends a detour. He wanted to have some time to be closer to his father and so he decided that instead of going around the mountain, they would climb over it.

"Are you serious Benjamin?"

"Yes, of course."

"It won't save us any time. It may even take more time for us to go all the way up to the top and back down again."

"I realize that. But this is what I need."

His friends shrugged their shoulders. They packed their food and belongings and prepared for their trek. As they began ascending the mountain, they could see a spark ignite within Benjamin. He was looking more rejuvenated with every step he took. He'd look up – up the mountain, up to the sky.

"I feel like I am closer to my father, that I get closer to him with every step I take."

When word spread that Benjamin had gone up into the mountain, many people who had trekked long distances to meet the Painter's son grew agitated. They didn't want to climb a mountain. Instead, they decided they would catch up with Benjamin on the other side. Everyone began to journey through the valley, crossing rivers and caverns for the chance to be there at the foot of the mountain when Benjamin returned.

Jeffery was one of the travelers. He was a much older man, had lived a very long life. He had attempted to do good deeds throughout his entire life. It had taken him a while to find the time to escape his life in order for him to learn more. From the first time he had heard about Benjamin, he had been unable to get his mind off of him. He was curious as to how much more he could learn from this amazing man.

As he approached the opposite side of the mountain, he was taken aback by the amount of people who had collected. Thousands of people were camped out at the base of the mountain waiting. It invigorated him to know that so many people had also felt this desire to find Benjamin and learn more about the painter.

Chapter 14

As Benjamin and his friends descended the mountain, they could see the gathering from afar. Danny was stunned. "How did they know you would be here?"

"Hopefulness, I guess," Benjamin smiled. Throughout his journey he had become inspired again. The mountain had helped clear his head, give him a new perspective to come up with a new message.

As he entered the crowd, Jacob, Danny and Max did their best to shield Benjamin from so many who just wanted to touch Benjamin. Who cried out for guidance, who wanted their futures told or health situations healed, or to see some sort of enchantment that only he could do?

Everything they had heard, every story about Benjamin had geared them up, primed them. They all stood there prepared to hear something amazing from the son of the Painter and Benjamin knew exactly what it was they needed to hear.

"Let us all gather for a feast!"

Danny turned to Benjamin and informed quickly in a hushed voice. "We don't have enough food to feed this many people."

Benjamin smiled and then announced to the crowd, "Could you believe that after everyone's journey, after everyone here has gathered, that my father wouldn't have found a way to feed us?"

There were murmurs in the crowd. They looked around and shrugged their shoulders.

"Does anyone have a large basket we could use so to pass out food to the crowd?"

A traveling basket maker stepped forward. "I do." He then crawled into the back of his truck and pulled out the largest basket he had ever made.

Max and Jacob gathered all of the food they still had with them and placed it in the basket. Then Benjamin stepped up to it.

"My father created this world from the need for perfection. He wanted a place that would always make him, and those within it, happy. From the rich soil, luscious plants, and the sky that rains and helps those plants grow and produce fruit, he created a world that provides for all.

While the people of his world, my other world, struggle and fight, work hard and go without, this world, the Painting, wasn't meant to be that way. I guess it wasn't until the people of our world invaded the Painting that their ideals tainted it.

Your currency wasn't meant to exist. You were supposed to collect your food, build your homes and tend to the animals. If you had too many bushels of apples you were supposed to share with neighbors. If you had a talent for building you were supposed to help those who didn't possess that skill. If you had a way with animals you were designed to assist those who couldn't care for my father's nature. And if your desire was to travel and never stay in one place, it was hoped that you would travel with extra surplus and spread the wealth of my father's bounty with those in areas that couldn't get it.

It's not about money, wealth or greed. It's about helping one another, being a part of something bigger. So, as I send this rather large basket through the crowd, full of all of the food we have left, I want you to take what you want. Feed yourself; feed the person standing next to you, and pass that basket on. I fully expect this food will fill everyone's belly here and then we can settle down with full bellies and readied ears to hear my message."

Jacob and Max glanced at each other, and then looked back at the basket they were holding. There was not much food in it. Definitely not enough to feed this crowd. The looks on their faces spoke this to Danny: "I trust that Benjamin knows what he's doing. The three of them carried the basket down to the crowd and handed it to the first person. It didn't take long until that large basket was encapsulated by the masses and no longer visible to them.

Benjamin sat down on a nearby rock and took a drink from his water canister. Danny and Jacob sat next to him as Max stood still attempting to catch a glance of the basket that had long disappeared. After a significant amount of time had passed, he saw the majority of the front of the crowd sitting on the ground eating and the crowd off in the distance was slowly, one by one, settling down for dinner themselves.

Max wanted to be amazed and awe-struck at how such a small amount of food could go so far. He finally returned to Benjamin and the others and sat down to join them.

"You are confused, aren't you?" Benjamin looked at Max knowingly.

"I trusted it would work..." he hesitated, "but don't know how."

"Do you need me to tell you what the people of the crowd figured out on their own?"

Max didn't want to admit it. He looked over at Danny and Jacob and could tell they already understood how it worked. How did they figure it out and he didn't?

"Some people in the crowd, I am certain, are in the same situation as you. They don't know how it happened; they just accepted it since they got fed. Others in the crowd KNOW how it happened because they helped to make it happen. Can you guess how?"

Max sat there in thought for a moment, when fragments of the story Benjamin had told earlier popped into his head. "They added to the basket?"

Benjamin nodded. "Sharing. Contributing your excess to those less fortunate, those who need it... We were designed, painted into this canvas to first and foremost be caretakers of my father's work. To nurture the animals, tend to the plants, and cultivate their bounty. It was a given with this task in mind, that we would care for our fellow man as well.

After dinner was over and the entire crowd's bellies were full, the basket maker's basket found its way back to him. When he looked inside, he still saw some food, and was just amazed at the phenomenal act that had happened today. How had Benjamin done it? How had he fed so many people with such a small amount of food?

He turned to someone sitting next to him. "Did you get enough to eat?"

"Sure did. Isn't Benjamin amazing?"

"You pulled your food from the basket?"

"Yes of course."

The basket maker turned to the person sitting next to the other stranger who had been listening. "You full, too?"

"Yes, and I got it from the basket. Aren't you full?"

"Well yes... but when the basket passed me by there wasn't much food in it. In fact, I'm almost sure that there's more food now, than there was earlier."

"Well there you go," replied the stranger.

The night sky was dark and clear. There were no clouds, no lights from nearby cities. As Benjamin looked up, he could see every star in the galaxy. As he stared at it, it reminded him of the view from his father's den. Of course, this view didn't include the Painting he always strained to see.

Straining now to look at each star individually, even the ones furthest away, Benjamin began to wonder if his father was looking at him from his chair. Could he see his son, this tiny speck on that tiny blue speck within that massive black canvas surrounded by millions of tiny white specks?

The universe his father painted to protect the Painting was enormous. Benjamin could just barely comprehend how large it truly was. From this small spot that he sat on, after traveling for so long and hardly making it very far at all compared to the mass of this colossal canvas, Benjamin's mind spun like the galaxy his father designed.

He was lost in his thoughts for who knows how long, when the crowd hushed. The silence attracted his attention and he looked out upon the massive group. They were all looking at him, as he stared up towards the sky. They were certain he was receiving a message; so they expectantly awaited him to say something.

With a deep breath, Benjamin stood and began to speak. "From my father's chair I can see this world, but it seems so far away. It's a tiny blue and green speck surrounded by so many white dots that I could never finish counting, and trust me I've tried on many occasions.

Look up at the sky. What do you see? Stars. Thousands of tiny shimmering stars completely surrounding us in the vastness of space. Can you count them? Has anyone ever tried? Has anyone ever traveled completely around the globe? It took us an entire day of walking to get here, and from my father's perspective, we hardly moved at all.

Did you know that what my father sees is very much like what we see when we look up at the night sky? We see stars that are bigger than others and some are smaller. Some are bright, some are dim, some are so small and so far away we can hardly see them, but we know they are there.

My father sees the stars we can't see. He sees the stars on the other side of the planet. He sees the stars that are so far away from us that we can hardly see them and yet, those stars are the biggest for him to see. The biggest stars to us, are the smallest stars for him.

The difference with what he sees, the biggest difference, is that from his chair, he also sees us. He sees this planet spinning around the sun, followed by planets that were designed to separate the Painting from the rest.

This world is the only world in that Painting that has these colors. The various hues of the blues, the large specks of green that dot across the curvature of the canvas, the browns of the land and the whites of the clouds that move along the outskirt, making a unique halo around the globe. It's a glow that helps this Painting pop off the canvas.

I mention this not to make you feel isolated and alone, but to help you realize how incredibly special you are. There are no other worlds as perfect, as purposely thought out and planned, as this one. My father put almost everything he had into this canvas to create us and then he used everything else to protect us.

When you think about it this way, when you consider life and you contemplate your purpose or speculate what might be out there, I want you to know in your heart how important you are. I want you to look up at the night sky in astonishment and admiration that my father, your painter, designed everything around us, including us.

We're all part of his plan. We are all exceptional and unique. We are loved more than we, as mere humans, can possibly fathom. Even with my knowledge, even with everything I have learned and taught, even with my own connection as being raised by your creator, I am still awestruck by his design.

Chapter 15

Over the course of many years, Benjamin traveled and shared his father's love with anyone who would listen. His three friends, Danny, Jacob and Max joined him.

Their journey was the longest, hardest and most tiring excursion they could have ever dreamed, and yet, it was the most rewarding as well. The three of them learned more about Benjamin's father than they could ever retell.

As the four of them turned the corner to the road leading to their home town, they felt the excitement begin to build. Seeing the outskirts, knowing they were almost home, lifted their spirits.

As they crossed the threshold of the town, they began getting recognized and word spread like wildfire.

"They're home!"

"Benjamin is home."

"The Painter's son has returned!

As they made their way down Main Street everyone emerged from their businesses and homes. They filled the streets and applauded and cheered. It was a wonderfully uplifting feeling. They were being inundated with questions from every direction.

"Where have you been?"

"What did you see?"

"What magical acts have you performed?"

Benjamin was almost too tired to answer. He smiled and waved, and when he felt as if his answers weren't going to be heard, he simply responded with, "Later."

A number of business owners sent their employees or their own children to the homes of the returnee's family. Before long, word got out to Benjamin's parents and they came running to see their son.

"My Son!" His mother, Miriam, exclaimed when she saw Benjamin standing on the street surrounded by the masses.

The crowds seemed to part to make way for Benjamin and he gladly ran to his mother. As they hugged, his father, Christopher, joined in. It was a wonderful reunion.

"I'm so glad you are home!"

"It's good to be home," Benjamin smiled.

"You must come for dinner tonight! A celebration of your return."

"And of course, bring your friends," his father added.

Franklin had been standing nearby in a dark alleyway. He chose to stay in the shadows and out of sight as the town crowded the street. When he saw Benjamin, his heart sank. Before Benjamin left for his journey, he gave Franklin his sketchbook with the hope that he'd deliver the pictures within.

Franklin never told Sammy about the sketch-book. He knew Sammy would not understand. He'd find a reason to belittle Franklin for thinking he was someone important. Or he'd put Benjamin down and take away and destroy the book, like he destroyed the picture Benjamin had given him the first night they met.

Although Franklin had tried, he had been unsuccessful in finding a single person from the sketchbook. He hadn't been able to deliver a single picture and it worried him that Benjamin would be disappointed. Yet, it wasn't for a lack of trying.

Franklin studied the pictures. He looked at the sketches every single night, memorizing the people, the facial features, the clothes. He didn't know them. He didn't recognize anyone, but he didn't ever want to come across them and not give them their picture. He put every picture to memory. Every sad face, every group, every loved one hugging one another. He saw dirty tear stained faces, and some had torn clothes. He always wondered if these people were homeless, but when he'd venture down to the homeless shelters, he never saw them.

That was another thing he never told Sammy. So he could get near the homeless people in hopes of finding those images from the pictures, he offered to volunteer. He handed out food in the soup kitchen, greeted people as they walked in the door and handed out clean blankets to those staying on cold nights.

Sammy never would have understood why Franklin was doing it. Franklin didn't even fully understand why he was doing it – but he knew it made him happy. He enjoyed helping others, but there was always a twinge of disappointment each night when he left and he hadn't handed out a single sketch.

Sammy sat fuming in the garage. He was watching sports and drinking but he was angry, a bitter fury was continuing to build within him each hour Franklin wasn't there.

Franklin wouldn't tell him where he spent his time. Sammy was certain Franklin had made other friends, although he hadn't any proof. He resented the idea that Franklin was going to move on with his life and leave him.

That night when Franklin walked in Sammy ignored him at first. The irritation he felt kept him from even acknowledging his friend's presence.

"Sammy, I'm here."

"What do you want? A medal?"

"I didn't think you heard me enter."

"Where were you today?"

"Running errands."

"What kind of errands?"

"Boring errands," Franklin lied, although with very little believability.

Sammy looked at him angrily.

"If you are going to lie to me, then leave. I don't need to see your ugly, fat face."

Franklin started to protest, but he stopped. He didn't like it when Sammy acted this way and he realized there was no reason to put up with it. Especially not tonight, when all he really wanted to do, was see Benjamin, even if he wasn't invited to the celebration dinner.

Franklin stood there looking at his friend for a long moment and suddenly realized, he didn't need to stay. He lowered his head, exhaled a brave breath, and then turned to leave. As the door closed behind him and he never heard his friend utter another word, he left feeling he had made the right decision.

Chapter 16

As Benjamin walked the pathway to his parent's house, he thought about all of the wonderful accomplishments he had made. He felt he had taught the people so much. He knew there were still tons of stories to tell, so much more information he could impart. So many opportunities awaited him right around the corner.

The sun was starting to set but it shined out brightly. The wind was whistling softly through the leaves of nearby trees and nightingales were singing. The day had turned out to be wonderful and tonight was going to be grand.

He was on his way to a celebration, a dinner meant for a king and he looked forward to just relaxing, hanging out with his friends and celebrating into the morning hours. What a great life he had.

"Son." A voice reverberated within his chest and nearly knocked him from his feet. "Son, please hear me."

"Father?" Benjamin spoke kneeling on the ground and looking up towards the sky. The sun was setting and yet it seemed to shine directly over Benjamin. The shadows surrounded him and he felt like a spotlight was shining on him.

"Son, heed my warning."

"I hear you Father."

"Heed my warning and know that the time has come and danger is on its way."

"Danger?"

"The end is drawing near. Something bad is coming and you need to be prepared."

"What do you mean Father?"

"I see and hear everything. Like the day I watched the inchworm, I can look down and see your pathway and the obstacles that are coming and I can't do anything to change it."

"What's going to happen?"

"What they do will be linked to what you do. You must follow the path that will be set before you and you must see it through to the very end."

"See what through? What's going on?"

"There are those who fear the unknown. Those that don't understand your gifts. They don't believe you are my son."

"They have free will, they don't need to." Benjamin spoke feeling as if something was off about his father.

"Yet they spend their efforts turning others against you. They're planning something horrible."

"I'll stop them. What should I do?"

"I can't tell you what to do Son. You must seek the answers on your own."

"But you know what is going to happen. Why can't you just tell me?"

"Because my worries for you will remove your ability to choose your own path."

"I'm not sure what I'm supposed to do."

"Be brave my dear son. You'll be coming home soon."

Benjamin shivered. *I'll be coming home soon?* He wondered as the silence filled his heart. *What did his father mean by that? Was he about to die? Was someone going to kill him? Why? Could he do something to stop this from happening? Should he?*

He watched the sun continue to dip down behind the hilltop and he witnessed the sky turn blood red. A terrifying fear swept through him as he kneeled onto the pathway and called to his father again.

As his adrenaline spiked his heart rate sped up. He found himself trembling. He had never felt this scared. Was this his father's doing, or was it fear of the unknown that terrified him? Nothing in his life had ever caused him to feel like this.

With no answer, Benjamin turned his heart outward to collect any will his father may have been sending. He felt the warmth of the day escape the land and he felt the bitter cold of the wind chill him to the bone.

He opened his eyes, worried, terrified, wishing he knew exactly what was coming, wanting to know how to prepare, how to stop it, how to fix it. He started to cry, when a bunny emerged from the tall grasses beside him.

He looked at the small white rabbit and smiled at it. It was curious about him. Its whiskers twitched but still it took tiny hops towards Benjamin and approached cautiously.

Benjamin recalled the story his father told him about the day he went into the Painting. He remembered the scene of the bunny that climbed onto his father's lap and tickled his nose with its whiskers.

He always loved that story. It reminded him of peaceful times, of simplicity, of love. It was reminiscent of how wonderful and enchanting the Painting was. How it fixed itself with rebirth and fresh life.

It was as if he were being told that everything would be okay. That even the aftermath of a great flood that destroyed so much could still bring life and joy.

Benjamin realized that the warning wasn't meant to stop him or frighten him, but to prepare him. To face what was about to come with dignity because it was going to be in this moment, his last moment, that would last for all eternity in the minds of those he loved.

Benjamin stood and continued walking towards his friend's house. He knew that a celebration was coming, they all needed it, and he knew that this would be his last chance to teach them one final lesson.

As he approached the door, the words were still forming in his head.

The door opened and arms reached out to grab him. They pulled him into the house, and the music and laughter began.

Chapter 17

Franklin may not have been invited, but he desperately wanted to hear what Benjamin may say. He sneaked in the back yard, climbed up the trellis, and squeezed his way in through the attic window.

As he slowly crawled out onto the rafters of the ceiling, he looked down upon the crowd gathered below. It was dark where he was, dusty, and felt far away. He looked down to a well-lit room, at a crowd of happy people, and smelled the aroma of the food waft up to him.

"To the man of the hour!"

Jacob held up a glass as everyone joined in. "To Benjamin! My best friend and the son of the Painter!"

Benjamin joined as everyone toasted, then all settled down in their seats. The words were still forming in his head but he knew he needed to get some of them out while he still could.

"May I have everyone's attention?" He tapped the side of his glass with a fork. "I have something to say."

Everyone quieted and looked over with adoration towards their friend. No one knew the fear he was feeling in his heart.

Benjamin took a deep breath. "You will have to bear with me; there is so much I want to say and so little time."

"Yes, we don't want the food to get cold," Jacob laughed with many others. Benjamin smiled, yet his facial expression showed the group that he had something important that needed to be said. They quieted again to listen.

"I have one last thing I need to teach you."

"One *last* thing?" Jacob asked aloud. "Are you going somewhere?"

Benjamin shrugged with a half-hearted smile. He didn't answer the question, but he did continue his thought.

"This is something very important to me. It is my desire that you may know my father as well as I know him - that these words may comfort you in times of sorrow."

"Sorrow? This night is for celebration!" A voice called out from across the room. Yet the majority of the room remained quiet. Something important was going on.

"This night will end soon and what comes next, no one can prepare for."

Someone coughed, but otherwise it was so quiet you could've heard a mouse squeak.

"Today was perfect, tonight will be great, but tomorrow isn't promised and we must take heart in remembering why."

Everyone knew Benjamin was letting on that something was coming. They began to wonder what he wasn't telling them.

Franklin, still straddling the rafters above, squirmed a bit closer so he could hear what Benjamin was about to say.

"My father, the artist of this universe - Geody he's been named. He painted this world and willed it to life. He made us all in his image."

Just then everyone heard a loud crack from above. They looked up and scrambled as Franklin fell from the rafters on the floor behind the table. Many of the men stood and ran to him. "Intruder!" They grabbed his arms and yanked him to his feet.

While Benjamin had been caught off guard by the intrusion, he recognized Franklin.

He understood why the man wanted to be here and he felt sad for him that he didn't feel wanted enough to come in through the front door.

"Let him go," Benjamin pled.

"But Benjamin he snuck in, he could mean you harm."

"He's trespassing." Those angry words filled the room.

"He should hear what I have to say too," Benjamin declared. "We should forgive those who interfere or impose upon us. They know not what we are facing in our lives. All they know is what is important in their lives. How would you feel, if you wanted to be included, if you crashed someone's party because you were so desperate to belong, and you were judged and kicked out? We are all one family in my father's eyes. You are all his children just as much as I am. He made you out of love and wants you all to love one another."

The men looked amongst each other, then hesitantly, released Franklin's arms. Franklin dusted himself off as one of the ladies grabbed a spare chair for him. As everyone sat back down at the table, Benjamin collected his thoughts.

"My father sent me here to teach you his will. He desires good from everyone but knows you each will be tempted towards evil. It is our will to choose our path. It is up to us to make the right choices, to do what is best for us, but also what will make my father proud.

What I want to remind you about is my father's love. It was his love that created this world. It was his love that brought you to life. And it was his love that sent me to you. He wants nothing but happiness for each and every single person on this world. If you just consider my father's will, if you stop to think about what is right and wrong, he will open your heart to doing the right thing. He is the king of all creation. He has the power to bring life. He is the glory, for now and forever. Remember this, all of you."

Benjamin sat down and bowed his head. With eyes closed and hands clenched together, fingers intertwined, he whispered just loud enough for all who strained to hear.

"Thank you, my father, for this food we are about to eat. May our lives bring you joy as we hold you in our hearts."

Benjamin looked up to the ceiling and closed his eyes. He listened to his father's silence, absorbed whatever it was his father wanted him to have and then looked back at the gathering of people at the table before him.

"What's going on Benjamin?" Jacob asked with worry in his voice.

"What's going on is we're about to have a meal together. Please pass the bread."

Chapter 18

The thanks of blessing was a first for anyone. It set the mood for an interesting evening. Dinner was incredible. The time with friends was a blessing to Benjamin. He even allowed himself to let go his worries long enough to enjoy the time they all had together.

Benjamin watched the hours tick by faster than a woodpecker's beak. Before he knew it many of their guests had left and he sat alone on the living room couch with his thoughts.

His father's warning repeated itself in his mind. Knowing the end was near terrified him. Not knowing what to expect or how to prepare left Benjamin's mind swirling with thoughts.

The room was dark, but there was enough light for Jacob to notice Benjamin sitting alone.

"Benjamin?" Jacob spoke low not wanting to startle him.

"Jacob, please sit with me. There is something I should tell you."

On the other side of town Franklin was making his way back home. Having heard what he had heard and witnessed the love of this family of friends, Franklin felt conflicted. He was angry he wasn't invited, but happy he was allowed to stay. He was lost in thought; his pace slowed.

"Where were you tonight?" Sammy stepped out of the shadows.

Franklin looked at him and felt a fear surge through his body.

"Don't bother trying to lie because I already know."

"Then why ask?"

Sammy stalked up to him, towering over him like a monster. "Did he mention where he was going tomorrow?"

This was one of those moments that tested what you were made of. Franklin knew Benjamin was acting weird tonight. The words he had said, his actions all reflected a person who knew something was coming. Had he known?

"I'm waiting," Sammy growled reminding Franklin his patience was running thin.

"There's a ballgame tomorrow afternoon."

During dinner Jacob presented Benjamin with a set of tickets to see the ball game tomorrow. Everyone was excited about this game. It was going to be the biggest most important game of the season. Most everyone in town was planning on attending.

The excitement throughout the streets was wild. Benjamin even began feeling the excitement himself. He wanted to experience this joyous event, this gathering of so many of his father's people. It felt like a happy place, a safe place. He even half-hoped that the warning his father gave him about tomorrow had been wrong and that tomorrow would be fine.

The entire town had gathered in the overly packed stadium. There was food and cheering, talking and excitement. The game was close; the score was tied most of the time. One team would score, then the other team would score. The crowd was on the edge of their seat. No one knew about the evil scheme Sammy had put forth.

After the halftime break, Sammy made Franklin go in and chain up all of the exit doors. While Franklin was preoccupied with his task, Sammy initiated phase two.

Franklin didn't know much of Sammy's plan. They still hung out together, but since Franklin's time with Benjamin, Sammy began keeping secrets. He was angry a lot, but kept Franklin close. It was an odd feeling, being needed but not knowing why.

After Franklin had locked the last door, he made his way back over to where he had left Sammy and was shocked by what he found.

"You can't do that!"

"Oh yes I can" Sammy scowled as he connected the last wire to the bomb.

"But you'll hurt people, kill people!"

"That's what I want to do."

"But why?"

"Why?" Sammy barked angrily. "How can you ask me why? They all treat us like scum. They hate us, judge us, want to lock us up and throw away the key."

Franklin was terrified. He didn't know what to do. He knew he couldn't let this happen. He lunged towards Sammy right as Sammy switched the power on.

Franklin knocked Sammy to the ground and held him there. "I won't let you do this. I'll turn you in myself."

"And I thought you were my friend!" Sammy struggled beneath the large man. "Well, you're too late." Sammy's face filled with an evil grin as he caught the panic in Franklin's eyes.

Franklin turned around to look at the bomb and saw the timer ticking down. He shook Sammy, "Turn it off!"

"No!" Sammy kicked Franklin off of him and jumped to his feet. "And now I know where your loyalties lie." Sammy towered over Franklin on the floor. "Now you'll suffer the same fate as all of them!" He kicked Franklin in the gut, then turned and ran towards the last remaining unlocked door.

Franklin struggled to get to his feet. He was fairly certain Sammy had just broken one of his ribs, but there was no time to check his wounds. He ran to the door to chase after Sammy but when he tried to pull it open, he felt it tug back and heard the rattle of chains. Sammy had locked him in.

Franklin turned back to the bomb and ran to it. He looked at all of the wires, a cluster of colors he couldn't even dream of deciphering. He didn't know how to turn it off and he was terrified if he tried, he'd trigger it.

The only thing he could think to do now was run to get help. He ran towards the first opening he could find into the stadium. He ran to the edge of the railing and over an enormous crowd talking, laughing and cheering. He yelled at the top of his lungs, "Where is Benjamin?"

People near him turned to look at him, some shrugged, some looked around.

"Benjamin, I need your help!" He yelled again, his voice cracking with terror.

"I'm here," came a voice from a seat a number of rows up. Benjamin stood so Franklin could see him.

Franklin was holding his side. He was visibly wounded and the look on his face was far worse than any fear Benjamin had ever seen. "The time – it's counting down!"

The word time echoed in Benjamin's head. His father's warning repeated and his stomach filled with butterflies.

"What's going on?" Benjamin inquired as the cameraman panned the view to Benjamin in the crowd and displayed him on the big screen.

"A bomb!

The people nearest to Franklin began to scream, while others a bit further, started to ask, "What did he say?"

"He said there was a bomb!"

"A bomb?" another screamed.

Benjamin realized within a fraction of a second that the entire stadium was going to fill with panic. He had to do something; he looked at the cameraman so his eyes were looking out at the entire stadium from the big screen and he spoke as calmly as he could.

"Everyone please stay calm. Cautiously make your way out to the exits. Do not push each other."

"They can't!" Franklin yelled. The camera-man spun the camera down to Franklin so everyone could hear and see. "All of the exits have been locked."

Women and children screamed. Panic was already taking over.

Benjamin called out as loudly as he could, the cameraman swung the shot back up to him. "I need the strongest men to be let through. Every man strong enough to break down a door, get to the closest exit and help the people escape."

Chapter 19

As everyone began moving, tears, cries of fear and panic filled the stadium. Benjamin quickly pushed his way down the stairs to Franklin and Franklin led him to the bomb.

They ran up to it, past panicked people waiting in terror for the larger men at the closest exit to do their job. Some were heaving their shoulders into the door to loosen it, while others were trying to find something to break it down. A woman broke an emergency fire case and pulled out an axe. It was hastily handed through the crowd to the men at the door, while another man grabbed a large metal trash can and began banging it against the exit lever, hoping it would break.

The people were working together to free themselves. If Benjamin would have been able to praise them, he would have, but he was looking at the bomb and feeling completely lost.

As doors opened and the light of the day shone into the dark crowded hallways, Benjamin started to rejoice. He turned to Franklin and demanded of him, "Help them out. Make sure everyone gets to safety."

"What about you?"

"Go! Save them!!" Benjamin demanded.

Franklin did what he was told. He turned to help the crowd. He helped up those who were smaller and weaker, who had gotten pushed out of the way or knocked over. He lifted many people off of the ground and got them to their feet again. He ran down the hall making sure everyone was getting help, and finding their way out.

Danny, Max and Jacob finally found their way through the crowd to Benjamin. They had no idea where he had gone, but knew in their hearts they needed to find him. As they ran up, Benjamin was fast at work disconnecting wires from barrels.

"How can we help?"

"Make sure everyone gets to safety!"

"We aren't going to leave you, Benjamin," Jacob declared.

"We're running out of time. These barrels are close together. If I can't disassemble all of them there will be a domino effect. The stadium is going to go down, and if it does, it will take everyone in it. You must help the people escape!"

Max and Danny both glanced at each other. They realized Benjamin was right. They each turned and ran separate directions back into the stadium to make sure no one had been left behind. Jacob however stayed with Benjamin. He watched what Benjamin did to withdraw a wire and ran to another barrel to do the same.

He looked at the barrel and was immediately overwhelmed. He couldn't recall which wire it was Benjamin had grabbed. He was flustered and couldn't make a decision. His hand hovered over each wire, he was reaching for one, any one to pull, when Benjamin took his hand in his.

"We've got to go!"

Hearing the words 'we' come out of Benjamin's mouth and being dragged towards the exit, Jacob felt relief. They ran towards the exit. It was a rectangular opening filled with light and two large metal doors lying haphazardly on the ground next to it.

Jacob and Benjamin were running at full speed, faster than Jacob had ever run his entire life and as he neared the light, he felt Benjamin's hand let go. Before he knew it Benjamin pushed him through the exit and then turned back towards the bomb.

With the speed Jacob was rushed through the door, it took him more than twenty feet to slow to a stop. By the time he was able to turn and try to find Benjamin with his eyes, all he saw was the dark shadow of his friend racing back towards the bomb with a large metal door width way in front of him.

As he started to take his first step back towards the stadium, the reddish orange flames came shooting towards him and the aftershock of the explosion threw him backwards another twenty feet.

He hit the pavement so hard his elbows, back and head felt as if he had been hit by a train. He looked up towards the opening and watched helplessly as concrete and metal came tumbling down into a pile.

"Benjamin!" he yelled, scrambling to get to his feet. He ran to the fallen rubble and began pulling away loose rocks.

"What's going on?" A couple of men approached.

"Benjamin was still inside."

They, too, immediately began helping to pull away the debris.

Others came up, they, too, joined in the task of removing debris. When there was an opening just large enough for Jacob to crawl through, he did. The others kept at their duty.

Jacob crawled over large chunks of fallen concrete and twisted metal support beams. "Benjamin," he called out, as he made his way to the last location he remembered seeing his friend.

When he saw the metal door, he slid to his knees and began to lift it. As he slid it away from his friend's body, he cried, "No, no, no, no, no! You can't be dead! You can't!"

Jacob kept removing debris off of his friend until he came to a mottled steel beam pressing his friend down. He tried with every fiber of his being to lift it and when it budged, Benjamin coughed.

"Thank Geody you're okay!"

Benjamin slowly opened his eyes and watched as his friend helplessly attempted to lift the metal beam but failed.

"Jacob..." Benjamin voiced through pained breathing.

Jacob kept trying to move the beam. He didn't want to give up although he knew in his brain there was no way he could lift this monstrous girder.

"My friend..."

"I've got to get this off of you."

"Jacob, you won't.... I've not long left in this world."

The tears burned Jacob's eyes and he tried again to lift the metal beam.

"Jacob, please stop."

Jacob stopped, but continued to look down at the beam, terrified to look at his friend, horrified that he was going to watch his friend die. "I can't move it."

"You aren't meant to."

The tears flowed down Jacob's face.

"My time has come..."

"No, Benjamin. You're going to be okay." Jacob cried as he turned to face his friend. "Others are coming, we'll get you out."

"I must tell you something."

Danny and Max had joined those removing debris until they, too, were able to get in. They crawled through the debris and called out for Jacob and Benjamin.

"We're over here," Jacob cried out.

They followed the sound to their friend and paused when they saw the scene. Max smacked Danny on the arm and he snapped out of it. They both ran to the metal beam and with both of their strength they attempted to lift it. It moved, slightly, but when it did, the sound of creaking metal and large boulders shifting filled the cavernous tomb. They paused.

"It's too late," they heard Jacob whisper.

They carefully released the metal beam and looked at Benjamin's lifeless body. His eyes were closed. He wasn't moving. All of the muscles in his face had relaxed. It almost didn't look like him.

Danny and Max fell to their knees next to Jacob. They wailed.

Two other large men came into the stadium and grabbed the boys by their arms. They lifted them to their feet and pulled them to the exit.

"We can't leave him!" Danny cried.

"The stadium is coming down. We've got to get you out of here."

"We can't leave him," Max echoed.

"He's already gone." Jacob stood and solemnly walked towards the exit; the others followed. Danny looked back and saw his best friend's body lying under the debris. He suddenly felt as if half of his heart was still there – that it might always be there.

As they crawled through the narrow opening of collapsed debris, everyone heard a snap. Then they heard a crackle.

"It's going to come down!" Someone nearby yelled.

The people outside grabbed the men's arms and with adrenaline pumping through their veins, they hauled the guys through the opening.

As everyone cleared the exit and ran, the final snap sounded from a structural beam collapsing, and the remainder of the stadium came tumbling down.

Chapter 20

Everyone screamed as the shockwave hit them and knocked them over. The dust cloud from all of the ground up dirt and crumbling concrete knocked them over. It took a fair amount of time for the dust to clear. There was silence as everyone stared at what used to be the stadium, was now a large pile of rubble.

A woman nearby Jacob was the first to speak. "Where is Benjamin?"

Jacob looked at the woman solemnly, feeling the eyes of everyone nearby turn to look at him. He shook his head sadly and with a shaky whisper, about all the voice that he could muster he spoke.

"Benjamin is dead."

The woman gasped and screamed, then covered her mouth as her husband took her into his arms. Cries and screams and shocked people inquiring and repeating what they heard spread deeper into the crowd of people.

"What did he say?"

"Benjamin is dead."

"Benjamin, the Painters' son? He's dead?"

"That's what he said."

"Was he in the stadium?"

"Was he trapped?"

Jacob felt he needed to add more to the dialogue, "He saved us. He used his own body to block the blast."

"He saved us."

"He blocked the blast."

"He got us to safety."

"He's a hero."

"He's our savior."

"He just walked past? Where?"

As word spread down the line through the mouths of emotionally distraught on-lookers. Weeping and crying filled the parking lot.

The conversations and murmurs grew louder. The sobbing and disbelief increased. No one wanted to believe it. Some adamantly refused to believe it while others threw in their own ideas.

"He's not dead. His father, the creator of our entire world, wouldn't have let his son die!"

"He's not dead?"

"I heard that Jacob said he was gone."

"Gone? His body's disappeared?"

"I'm sure it's still there."

"What is?"

"His body, I heard he's walking around."

"Where? Where's the Painter's son?"

"He's gone."

"He's somewhere."

"Have you seen him?"

"I heard he was just here."

"He's around here somewhere."

"Benjamin is all around us now!"

Just then a low rumble filled the sky and the town quieted. A light rain shower blanketed them and moistened the ground.

"It's his father, crying..."

Jacob heard the people talking, their fears and confusion, their questions and answers. He felt he needed to correct them, to try to speak to them, but he was so devastated. The last scene of Benjamin's life kept repeating over and over again in Jacob's head.

Jacob sat on his knees holding Benjamin's hand. He watched helplessly as Benjamin slowed his breathing and closed his eyes. With his last breath he spoke three last words.

"It is done."

As Benjamin's last breath escaped his body, Jacob felt it go through him. It filled him with hope and faith. It was as if Benjamin's being touched his soul. And yet, as it escaped, it also filled him with an ever-growing anxiety that he was now alone. That the world was never going to hear another insightful message from the painter's son again.

As the crowd accepted the news, people just held each other. Their faces looked so sad. They hugged one another and held hands. It was a quiet, somber time.

As Franklin looked out amongst the crowd, he felt so guilty. He hadn't planned it, but he had helped make it happen, unknowingly. He scolded himself silently for not asking more questions, for trusting Sammy.

At first, he didn't make eye contact with the crowd. He hoped he wouldn't get in trouble or that the crowd wouldn't punish him for Sammy's acts, but he fully expected it to happen, and he knew he'd accept his punishment like a man. But then a little girl approached him.

"Sir, are you okay?"

Franklin looked down at her. She looked so concerned. He knelt down to her height and spoke, "Are *you* okay?"

"I am. I was just concerned about you. Your head is bleeding." She reached towards his head as he, too, placed his palm on the side of his face that he hadn't realized was throbbing, until now. When her little fingers touched his hand, a flutter tickled his heart. He looked at the girl carefully and then all of a sudden, he recognized something.

"I think I have something for you," Franklin said calmly, except inside him, the excitement was about to burst. He swung his backpack around to his front and opened it. He pulled out Benjamin's sketchpad and flipped to the page he recognized. It was a scene of a small girl reaching over to a man kneeling before her. He never realized in all of this time that the man in the picture was himself.

He tore the picture out of the sketchbook and handed it to the girl. She took it and stared at it, as her mother approached and looked at it as well. Her father joined them, and held his wife and they both looked at the girl as she turned to show them her picture.

When the parents recognized the picture was one of Benjamin's sketches, the mother gasped. She began crying and calling out thanks to Benjamin.

"Thank you, Benjamin. Thank you for being a part of our lives."

Other's nearby heard her, and in hearing Benjamin's name, approached hoping that he was there, that the news of his demise was inaccurate.

Franklin watched as the people gathered. A small group approached the woman and with hand gestures they asked where Benjamin was. They pointed towards the stadium as another couple hugged. Franklin recognized this scene as well and as he flipped to that page in the sketchbook and found it, he ripped it out and handed it to the person who initially asked about Benjamin.

"Benjamin is still blessing us with his gifts!" Someone exclaimed.

A restaurant owner walked up to Franklin. He had been watching the young man and was quite proud at what he was doing for the people. He gave Franklin a hug.

"Why?" Franklin asked, feeling the emotions whelping up within him.

"Because you listened to the message."

Chapter 21

The cries and screams of the people lifted up from the crowd like a chorus filling the skies. The sound trailed off farther and farther until it escaped the planet, the universe, and then, the Painting.

From a distance, Benjamin could hear the crying of the people and slowly opened his eyes. He looked around the room and felt confusion. He didn't seem to recognize where he was.

"My son..."

"Father?" Benjamin questioned as he looked over at his father sitting on a chair across from him. But it wasn't the father he had grown accustomed to seeing, it was his real father. When the confused look on his face morphed into a tired smile, his father spoke.

"Welcome home, Son."

Benjamin looked at the room, the familiar furnishings that he knew of more than a lifetime ago. It reminded him of his childhood, his first childhood; of hearing about the Painting and always wanting to go into it, to experience life within it. Then he remembered his life inside. His friends, his family, what had just happened; he suddenly began to cry.

"What is wrong, Son?"

"I failed you."

"Failed me? Son, you didn't fail me."

"I didn't accomplish my task. I wasn't able to fix things. I wasn't able to turn everyone's hearts towards you."

"Son, you could never fail me."

"What do you mean? They killed me, Father. They refused to listen."

"Many heard you Son. Many continue to hear your word and spread your message."

"I need to go back!" He sat up in bed.

"Why?"

"I should explain more. There's more to say, more information I could give. I shouldn't have left them like that, the way I did. They are heartbroken and lost. Can't you hear them?"

"I hear them, Son. Do you?"

"Of course I do. They are crying, wailing. They are lost and confused. Their hearts hurt..."

"Is that all you hear?" Gerald inquired.

"What else is there?"

A sly smile glimpsed Gerald's face. "Find Franklin's voice."

Benjamin quieted his mind to search for one voice within many. It took him a few moments of really focusing his attention but then he heard it.

"You will pay for what you did," Franklin growled angrily at Sammy.

"What I did? You were just as much a part of it as I was," Sammy came back.

"You didn't have to kill him."

"That was the only way to stop him. Now they will cry and move on and forget about him, we can all finally move on."

"Forget about me?" Benjamin's heart broke. "I worked so hard. I spent so much time with them. How could they forget?" Benjamin wanted to cry.

"Keep listening," his father spoke calmly.

Time speeds by much faster within the Painting. By the time Benjamin found Franklin's voice again another day had passed.

"I may not have known what Sammy was planning but I take responsibility for being a part of it. I locked the doors to keep everyone in so I need to be punished for my part."

"You can't!" Someone from the crowd cried out. "He's Benjamin's messenger. He shared Benjamin's sketches with the crowd. He helped to change so many lives."

"He also helped to hurt so many people."

"But everyone got out. No one died! It was a miracle."

"It was because Benjamin saved everyone. He's the hero, the savior, not Franklin."

Benjamin closed his eyes. His heart pained for Franklin. He could feel the man's guilt overwhelm him. He could also feel how much Franklin just wanted to do the right thing. He just wanted to be a good person. He had always wanted to do the right thing, but he was weak and just needed a good leader.

Benjamin didn't want this one act, this trust in a friend who didn't deserve it, to ruin a man who could do so much good in his life. He wished so hard that he could be there, that he could do something to help, that he could say something on behalf of Franklin... then before he knew it, he was standing in the Painting.

On-lookers gasped.

"Benjamin? Is this you?"

Benjamin looked at the crowd and smiled. He took Franklin's hand and then gazed at the on-lookers. "Love one another."

"What if we can't?"

"Forgive him," he continued.

"How can we?"

"It is what I want."

The people looked at Franklin whose eyes were as wide and filled with light and hope as any had ever seen. When they turned back to Benjamin, he was gone.

When Benjamin opened his eyes, he was back at home. His father was smiling at him.

"You are an amazing young man," he spoke proudly to his son.

Benjamin listened as a small group of his friends continued to tell the story about him. Over time their numbers grew. Those people told others. The word of Geody and his son blanketed the land. The creator is out there, watching over us, loving us." He accomplished what he came here for.

It took many, many generations, but the word stretched over the land. More and more people found a love for Geody and his son, Benjamin. Yes, there were still others who were against him, doubters, but the numbers who wanted the life Benjamin spoke of, continued to grow.

"One day Son you may need to go back. One day you may need to give them hope again. But since you've already been there, since you were born into the Painting, you will always have the power to go back. You can go back whenever you want to. You have the power now. They talk of you as much as, if not more than, they talk of me. In fact, many of them consider us one."

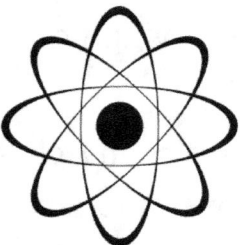

Ephesians 2:10 God has made us what we are and... he has created us for a life of good deeds, which he has already prepared us to do.

Who am I to write this story?

I ended the first book with this question and my answer was basically a dissertation of how I listened to God who led me. So now again, I find the need to ask this question. *Why me?* Because I wrote the first book and someone needed to write the second? That doesn't seem like a good enough answer.

I'm not a bible scholar, and recently I've felt out of place at church. I'm close to God, I feel as if **He** is my best friend – if you know me, you can understand how important that phrase "best friend" truly is... so the conflicting feeling I was experiencing; that church wasn't where I needed to be, caught me completely off guard.

I feel God everywhere. I look back and know which times in my life he walked with me.

I see his signs and hear his messages, because we ALL can, if we try. However, church is the primary place you are supposed to go for God – right? Church is where I met God for the first time in my adult life. Church was the place I felt most at home; it was warm and inviting and filled with the love of a God I was hungry to get to know.

So why was it, these past years, that I was feeling pushed to go somewhere else? And pushed is definitely the correct word. I'd love to say I was being pulled, that God was taking me by the hand and pulling me towards something better – but I can't. He wasn't there in the church for me... and I could feel that emptiness deep down within my soul.

Now, I'm not saying leave your church. If you are happy and you feel His love there, or you are getting the insight and education you need there, then that is exactly where you need to be. It is where I needed to be for so long absorbing his word like a sponge.

What I'm saying is God was my teacher. He educated me, showed me how to love and then sat quietly and watched me as I took the test. My test being, writing this book.

But it wasn't simply sitting at a desk and referring to the Bible. No, my test took me across the country. It introduced me to new people, it reminded me of old. It brought me closer than I could ever dream with someone whom I lost shortly after genuinely getting to know them. And then, I turned the page and realized the test was only going to get harder.

It tested my faith, and made me grow stronger. It showed me that I had that strength within me. That life is not easy, we are meant to work hard, but the rewards are worth it. This test gave me the inspiration to finish this story.

Sometimes God tests us.

Will we take the test, or will we walk out of the classroom?

Acknowledgements:
To New Friends

Conversations about faith, sharing God's love and reminiscing of our cherished loved ones whom are no longer with us. You fed me at that dining room table, body and soul. You listened, and gave me the opportunity to express myself when I thought no one was listening. You know who you are, because we are positively connected.

To my Grandfather who I was so blessed to have gotten to know in his end times. Whose scientific skepticism led me on a trek to understand and see God's love at work. Who reached for Jesus with his dying breath confirming that God loves us all and He always answers prayers.

The Pastor who suggested a book two which helped open my eyes to the possibility of this story becoming a trilogy.

To my readers, editors, narrator and fans who kept inquiring about this book and lighting a fire under me to finish it.

God works in mysterious ways.
It's not a cliché if it is true.

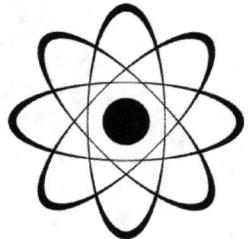

The Painting
3

Benjamin lived two lives – a life growing up with the Painter of a universe; someone to teach him about the wondrous possibilities there could be – and a life born into that enchanting world; growing up seeing first hand all of the miracles his father bestowed.

When he returned, he too heard the people just like his father. He heard their joy, and he heard their cries. It took him quite a long time to adapt to the changes in his life – but adapt he did.

Gerald encouraged his son, Benjamin, to venture out, to explore the world he had long forgotten; *their* world. Before too long Benjamin found a friend; someone who understood him, who became his wife and gifted him with a child. The day he held his newborn daughter, Nevaeh, in his arms was one of the happiest of his life.

Now that Benjamin was a father, he developed more appreciation for what his own dad had done for him. He described the beauty, the precision of all that worked within the Painting. He shared his experiences, all of the wonderful surprises his father gifted those beings with. These stories fascinated little Nevaeh. Every time they visited her grandfather she would race to his study to stare at the Painting. When she turned old enough, Gerald gave it to her.

Her desire to see what her father had seen, to be a part of what her grandfather had created, grew. She wanted so strongly to experience the love and majesty within the Painting, that her spirit found a way.

It was the love within her soul that got her into the Painting. It was that love of everything within, that kept her going back. And it was the love she shared within the Painting – that opened hearts and minds.

Her spirit was exactly what the Painting needed to heal the damage that had taken place.

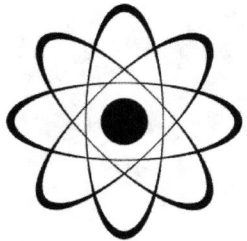

About the Author

Kathleen J. Shields is an award-winning author having won First Place Best Educational Children's Series from the Texas Association of Authors for "The Hamilton Troll Adventures".

The Hamilton Troll series is educational and inspirational, teaching young children social skills, animal characteristics and how to handle real-life situations.

While awaiting illustrations, Shields' writes chapter books for her slightly older readers. While still infusing education into each story, Kathleen endeavors to entertain young readers, igniting a desire to read that will span a lifetime.

Shields' also runs a website and graphic design company called Kathleen's Graphics. She designs colorful, eye-catching websites, logos and advertisements for businesses and authors. She enjoys being challenged to learn new things.

Additionally, Kathleen writes an inspirational and educational blog regarding her endeavors as an author as well as a business woman and Christian. Her views are always light-hearted and thought-provoking and are intended to get the reader thinking.

For more information about the author, and her books, please visit:
www.KathleensBooks.com
or follow her blog at:
www.KathleenJShields.com

More Great Books by this Author

Ghost Dogs

As a toddler Jamie develops an amazing gift, the ability to see Ghost Dogs. They look just like our past pets, just a bit more transparent.

Dream World Defenders

Ryan and his friends enter the dream world where they can do anything they can imagine – the only thing they can't figure out how to do? Wake up.

Constellation Crimes

A Giant Scorpion, a Crab Attack and a Killer Wolf – What do these have in common? The zits on Jared's face! A boys will be boys with active imaginations, story.

Ally Cat, A Tale of Survival

Allison Catsworth gets knocked off of a cliff and instead of falling to her death, she transforms into a cat and lands on all four paws!

A Rainbow of Thanks

Kate walks into a rainbow and is transported to various places on the planet as she tries to get back home.

The Painting

Gerald is given a blank canvas, so he paints a world, one that he loves so much – it comes to life!

The First Book of a Trilogy

Dandy Lion, A Legend of Love & Loss

Dandy loses a strand of hair each time he helps someone. He sews the seeds of love by doing good deeds.

The Dog Who Cried Woof

Riley takes it upon himself to announce Daddy's return home, but turns it into a game that goes horribly wrong.

Short Story eBook

Ethan's Reception

FiFi was not happy the day Ethan was brought home from the animal shelter... but Ethan was enthralled!

Short Story eBook

Also be sure to check out
The Hamilton Troll Adventures

And for Young Adults:
The Kaitlyn Jones Trilogy

CRIN GO BRAGH
Publishing

Has published various genres of books for numerous authors. Their portfolio consists of a 1200 page Vietnamese to English Dictionary, an award-winning children's series, multiple adult novels and memoires as well as Christian fiction. Their objective is to promote literacy and education through reading and writing.

www.ErinGoBraghPublishing.com
Canyon Lake, Texas

www.ingramcontent.com/pod-product-compliance
Lightning Source LLC
Chambersburg PA
CBHW061201170626
46809CB00003B/1202